Above
the
Llano

Look for other Western & Adventure novels by
Eric H. Heisner

Along to Presidio

West to Bravo

Seven Fingers a' Brazos

T. H. Elkman

Mexico Sky

Short Western Tales: Friend of the Devil

Wings of the Pirate

Africa Tusk

Fire Angels

Cicada

Conch Republic, Island Stepping with Hemingway

Conch Republic - vol. 2, Errol Flynn's Treasure

Follow book releases and film productions at:
www.leandogproductions.com

Above the Llano

Eric H. Heisner

Illustrations by Al P. Bringas

Visit our website at
www.leandogproductions.com

Illustrations by: Al P. Bringas

Dustcover jacket design: Dreamscape Cover Designs

Edited by: Story Perfect Editing Services – Tim Haughian

Hardcover ISBN: 978-1-956417-04-3

Printed in the United States of America

Dedication

To the land, which inspires.

Special Thanks

Amber Word Heisner, Al P. Bringas
& Clayton Leverett

The adventure continues from

West to Bravo
&
Seven Fingers a' Brazos

Note from Author

Fictional characters are like old friends. After each visit, you want to come back, see them again and share more time. This story came from my transition to the Texas Hill country. There are lots of places to explore and fuel the imagination: places like Enchanted Rock, the Longhorn Caverns, or just the many sandy creeks that finger their way across the landscape. These unique natural attractions have tons of history. For me, the stories of the Texas Rangers, out on an untamed frontier, sparked my interest.

Join Holton Lang on another adventure as he makes his way in a life full of uncertainties, in a land filled with danger. If you enjoyed *West to Bravo* and *Seven Fingers a' Brazos*, this will be a gathering of some familiar faces. Welcome back…

Eric H. Heisner

April 9, 2022

A lone horseman travels westward into the afternoon sun. Holton Lang keeps his mount moving along at a steady gait while scanning the landscape, being alert to his surroundings. A pair of birds flitters in the brush drawing his attention, though he maintains his riding pace.

Chapter 1

Holton stops his mount in a secluded spot near a rocky outcropping, where a campfire wouldn't be easily noticed. Feeling more alone than usual, without the company of his loyal canine or the recent travel companions, Holton draws out his big-loop rifle from the saddle scabbard and lets his gaze linger on the horizon once more. After a quiet moment, he slides his feet back from the stirrups, swings a leg over the horse's withers and drops to the ground with a soft thud.

Standing beside his mount, he loosens the cinch strap and undoes the saddle rigging. With the leather fastenings hanging free, Holton takes in his peaceful surroundings once more before tugging the saddle and tack from his horse and dropping it to the ground. He pulls the woolen blanket from beneath the saddle skirting and shakes it out before laying it over the cantle to dry in the sun.

~*~

Seated on the horse blanket next to a small fire, Holton leans over to grab his saddle bags and pull them nearer. Lifting the flap, he draws out a canvas sack and takes a piece of hard tack from inside. As he reclines against the pile of saddle gear behind him, he takes a bite and quietly chews.

1

Turning his contemplation from the light of the fire, Holton patiently lets his eyes adjust to the approaching night. He looks to his horse munching at the grass beneath a nearby, low-slung bush. His gaze travels down to the leather hobble ties on the horse's forelegs, and he nods, contented in knowing the animal won't be ranging far.

The glow of the evening sky continues to fade and nocturnal creatures announce themselves with calls into the cool desert air. Holton scans the adjacent rocks and foliage, while his surroundings slowly transition to mere shadows. The light from the fingers of flame in the campfire flicker off the scant items in camp, and Holton finishes his meal.

A lonesome expression, full of remorse, lingers on Holton's features, as he thinks back to his recent departure from the orphaned boy, Jules Ward, and his final goodbye. Memories of the cold stare of disappointment, and the terse farewell from the boy gives Holton an awkward pang of guilt. He thinks of the young man, that he treated like a son, and a moist glistening appears in the grown man's eyes.

Howls and yipping from a pack of coyotes breaks Holton from his reminiscing, and he instinctively looks around the camp for his dog. The scruffy, mongrel is nowhere to be seen. Holton turns away from the crackling firelight to stare out into the darkening night sky, uttering, "That's right, Dog... You just stay with that boy and keep him safe."

The overwhelming sense of being alone is evident, as Holton lets the small fire burn down and reduce to embers. Finally, he lies down on the horse blanket, props his head on the saddle rigging behind him and stares up into the stars. With his holstered pistol rolled in the cartridge belt at his side, and his big-loop rifle tucked-in close, Holton prepares to drift off to sleep. He places his hat over his face, adjusts the brim,

and murmurs a remembered saying to himself. "All is well…
Freedom is just the ability to endure loneliness."

~*~

Stirring with the predawn chill, Holton opens his eyes
before the first light of daybreak. As he pushes his hat up from
over his eyes, he can smell the burnt ash of the night's fire.
Flexing his stiff fingers to get the blood flowing, he tips his hat
further back on his head and sits up.

The landscape glistens and is heavy with morning dew.
All is quiet and still, as Holton shrugs off the cold and gives a
shake of his buckskin-clad shoulders. The hand-cut fringe
along his arm drips with moisture, and the cooler parts of the
leather touch his warm skin beneath. Seated with his rifle
across his lap, Holton reaches out with a stick to poke the
campfire ash in the hope of rekindling a flame.

The unusual quietness at the early hour of the new day
is unsettling. Holton scans his limited view of the landscape
and listens intently to the hushed silence all around him.
Realizing that he has halted his breath in an attempt to hear
something, he heaves a sigh of disappointment. Rifle in hand,
Holton rises to his feet and gives one more probing gaze to the
horizon before muttering to himself. "Gonna have to train me
a new dog…"

~*~

The sun coming over the horizon shines bright.
Walking in a wide circle around the perimeter of the camp,
Holton makes his way through the brush and scraggly trees.
Eyes studying the ground, he searches for his horse's trail and
comes across the short, hobbled stride of the hooved animal.
Looking up to the empty horizon again, the buckskin-clad
Westerner pauses and listens for any telltale sounds.

A heavy silence is all around. Holton's gaze returns to the ground, and he follows the trail a short distance to find a pair of moccasin tracks crossing the hoof prints of his mount. Taking a knee, Holton assesses the size of the man's track and mutters under his breath. "Damn…"

The underbrush scrapes against Holton, as he follows the commingled tracks of his horse and the sneaking Indian. Finally, he comes upon the loose set of leather hobble straps. Scanning the skyline while he listens, Holton picks up the leather ties and continues to follow the trail along until the prints of the moccasins disappear and the horse tracks deepen. Holton stops to look back in the direction of his camp. Inhaling deeply and releasing a slow sigh, Holton grumbles, "Now I got to get me a new horse."

Chapter 2

Boot soles skim across the sandy, rock strewn terrain, stepping lightly on the path they follow. With his rifle in one hand and his saddlebags draped over his opposite shoulder, Holton trails his pilfered horse. Pausing at a patch of slick rock where the tracks disappear, he scans the area and then picks up the trail again as it leads to the west.

~*~

The afternoon sun moves toward the western horizon. Behind a rock formation, Holton crouches down to observe a small Indian camp in the far distance. He waits and watches as the group of five Apache lounges about while talking and laughing. One of the braves stands before the others and seems to act out the scenario of stealing a horse in the night.

Beyond the Apache campsite, a dozen Indian ponies graze peacefully. Some untamed mustangs are mixed amongst the gentled horses wearing riding halters. Easy to pick out, being almost a head taller than the others, Holton's own large-boned gelding stands with the herd. Gripping his rifle in one hand and his saddle bags in the other, Holton quietly makes his way in a wide arcing path around the perimeter of the camp toward the group of horses.

Staying low and moving quietly, Holton creeps up on the herd of animals while keeping a watchful eye on the Apaches in the camp. He tucks his rifle and saddlebags under a bush and draws his knife from the sheath on his belt. Moving from one horse to the next, careful not to disturb them, Holton slices the rawhide ties on their feet.

As he approaches one of the hobbled mustangs, it snorts a warning, causing the other animals to skitter away with apprehension. Holton drops to his belly and keeps still. From his low vantage on the ground, he watches the Indian camp as the Apache turn their attention to the livestock.

One of the braves stands, picks up a carbine rifle and starts to walk toward the horses, intending to get a closer look. All is quiet, as the animals settle back into grazing and the approaching Apache puts a scrutinizing eye on the ponies. Stopping a few feet from the herd, the brave sees the wild mare that had put up the alarm, kick out and bite at another. He turns back to the camp and calls out to the others in a mix of Spanish and Apache. "*Es nada...* Just that canyon mustang we caught yesterday making trouble again." Casting his gaze over the herd again, the Apache waits a moment before lowering his rifle and returning to camp.

Beads of sweat form and trickle down Holton's cheek, as he lies in the scrub brush with only his knife for defense. He slowly lets out his held breath and glances at the lone Apache returning to the camp. Careful not to let his gaze linger too long, he remains still to keep from alerting the warrior to his presence.

The brave returns to the others to hear the rest of the horse-theft tale, and Holton turns to look at the wild mustang. He murmurs under his breath, as he creeps to the next animal. "If you're like that, I'll let you stay and learn some manners."

Above the Llano

After slicing the leg ties on several more animals, Holton makes his way back to his rifle and saddlebags.

~*~

The young Apache finally finishes his exciting account of fearless theft, and stands proudly before the others. Unexpectedly, the rest of the warriors rise to their feet and stare at something beyond the young storyteller's shoulder. Confused by their reaction to his thrilling tale, he studies them momentarily, and then turns to see what they are looking at. The five Apache braves look toward the grazing herd to see a white man with a U.S. Cavalry hat and fringed buckskin shirt sitting astride the larger gelding.

Holton raises his big-loop rifle, high, over his head. Mounted bareback, with his saddlebags across his lap and his lever-action gun held in the air, Holton bursts out with his facsimile of an Apache war cry. Punctuating the bold warning, he fires a single shot into the sky.

At the sound of the gunshot, the surrounding ponies, with the exception of the canyon mustang which still has the hobble ties on its legs, scatter in all directions. Holton gives the big-loop rifle a one-handed, twirling cock and stares commandingly at the astonished group of Apache warriors. He fires off a second shot from his rifle to ensure that all the animals are scattered, far and wide.

The braves stand silent, as they watch from the camp. The solitary man on horseback nods with satisfaction and gives a wave before turning his horse and loping away. Completely flummoxed, the braves turn to the youngest of their group, who merely shrugs his shoulders with an expression of uncertain guilt.

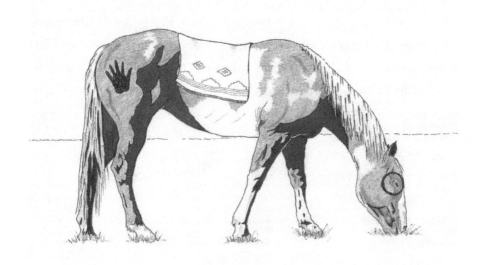

Chapter 3

Returning to his camp from the night prior, Holton recovers his saddle tack and blanket roll. He scans the empty horizon, keeping a watchful eye for anyone following. Unconsciously, he looks down at his side to where the loyal canine was habitually positioned and mutters. "Where were ya, Dog? You're usually at my heels for this sort of business…"

Holton slides his rifle into the saddle scabbard and lifts his boot to the stirrup. He steps up and swings a leg over the cantle to find his position in the saddle. All the while, his steady gaze scans the rocks of the surrounding landscape. "Dammit… I don't know which is worse? Talking to myself, or conversing with an Indian-sniffing dog…"

He shakes his head to clear the thought, clenches his spurs to the animal's flank and urges his horse onward along his westerly path. As he travels through the high desert landscape, Holton keeps his eyes trained on the low range of hills ahead. The heat of the day causes beads of sweat to run down Holton's back, creating dark lines on his buckskin shirt. He travels onward, his mind occupied with a longing for the cooler temperatures of higher elevations.

~*~

Through Texas and on to the Arizona Territory, the wide open spaces of sunbaked ground and scrub brush become clustered with undulating hills and rock formations. Holton carefully maneuvers his horse through a dip in the terrain and comes up from the gully to face a group of boulders. As he makes his way around the rock outcropping, his horse snorts an anxious warning.

With trepidation, Holton holds his horse in check, quietly listening a moment, then proceeds. Coming around the bend, he is suddenly confronted by five Apache braves. The familiar riders sit their mounts side by side, blocking the trail. Holton eyes the natives and groans under his breath. "Thanks for the warning, Dog."

Holton halts his horse to face the war-painted Indians. He notices that one of the Apache braves, sitting astride the green-broke canyon mustang, holds on with some difficulty. The group silently stares at the lone rider, until one of them prods his horse forward while calling out in his native tongue. "You…! Man-who-scatters-herd-to-the-wind…! You will give us your big horse and long gun!"

Holton holds his position and purposefully reaches down to draw out his big-loop rifle from the saddle scabbard. He places the butt of the rifle stock against his upper thigh and calls loudly to the warriors in their own Apache language. "I only take back what is mine and scatter your ponies to the wind as a warning."

The lead Apache looks back to his companions, who are equally surprised at the white man's familiar use of their speech. The foremost rider turns to Holton again and addresses him. "You speak with the Apache tongue?"

"I once lived among your kind."

"What is it you call yourself?"

Above the Llano

Feeling the nervous energy of the situation escalating, Holton keeps his restless horse in check and responds calmly. "My white-father gave me the name of Holton Lang."

The name seems unfamiliar to all the braves but one. Holton waits, watching as the lead rider is ushered back to the others for a brief powwow. He studies his opponents and recognizes the youngest of them as the horse-thieving storyteller. Smiling to himself, Holton notices that the young brave is stuck with the task of riding the untrained mustang. There is a brief shaking of heads and then, finally, a mutual agreement. The leader turns his horse to Holton and calls out. "You... The one called Holton Lang. Give us your long gun and horse, and you may walk away."

Holton reaches the rifle out to arm's length and gives the lever action a spinning twirl-cock. The rife goes around, comes back to him, and he rests the stock on his thigh again. Staring at the five mounted Apache, Holton sits quietly and readies himself for the coming fight. The braves stare at him, until their leader calls out in Apache. "You no leave alive?"

Unmoving, Holton responds in a mix of both tongues. "No... If you fight me, *you* no leave here alive."

The Apache all seem to understand Holton's warning very clearly and cast uncertain gazes amongst themselves. Eventually, after a long, hesitant pause, the lead brave raises up both his hands and lets out a challenging war whoop. Following his lead, the other Apache warriors lift their guns in the air and prod their horses forward.

Holton stands his ground, drops the barrel of his rifle to aim at the nearest rider, and fires a shot. The leading Apache takes the bullet hit to the heart and tumbles backward over the flank of his pony. Before the body hits the ground, Holton levers his rifle and fires on the next advancing rider. At the closing distance, that rifle shot also hits its mark, and the Apache warrior spins from atop his galloping pony. Without dropping his aimed sight from down the rifle barrel, Holton quickly levers the gun again and shoots another brave off his horse.

The sudden gunfire puts the canyon mustang into a fit of wild bucking, and the youngest warrior tries to hold tight. Holton levers his rifle again and turns his aim from the bronc-riding exhibition to the final mounted Apache. The remaining brave wisely brings his horse to a skidding halt, looks around at his three rifle-shot companions and then to the other sailing through the air after being bucked off. Deliberately, he throws his rifle to the ground and lifts his open palms skyward.

His cheek pressed to the rifle stock and his aim still trained on the last native horseman, Holton waits… He utters, "Not all have to die today…" The Apache lowers his hands, backs up his pony a few short steps, and nods his head in agreement. He reaches out to grab the halter on one of the loose horses and waits, as the young warrior climbs to his feet, dusts himself off, and jumps astride. Humbled, the two unarmed surviving Apache face their adversary.

Holton deliberately lowers his aim and holds the big-loop rifle across his chest. He lifts his right hand from the rifle's receiver and, as a sign of peace, holds up his open palm. The two Apache look to their fallen companions and turn their ponies to ride away.

After waiting a while for the pair of warriors to disappear into the distance, Holton prods his horse forward. Stepping past the dead men lying in the dirt, he shakes his head, muttering, "It is too bad we are the way we are." Directing his gaze to the empty trail ahead, he remains alert for another possible encounter with the retreating Apache. Holton looks down at the unoccupied spot alongside his horse's foreleg and murmurs to himself. "Sure wish I had that darned dog along 'bout now."

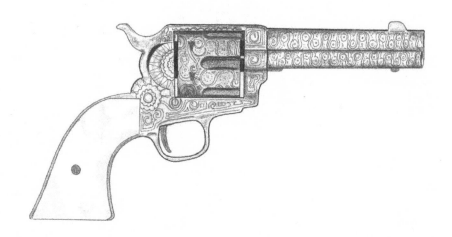

Chapter 4

On the south side of Austin, a pair of Texas Rangers walks out from a crowded saloon and strolls down the boardwalk. As the two rangers, Hobbs and Bentley, are engaged in lively conversation, the adolescent boy, Jules Ward, steps from around the corner to follow after them. Having discarded his worn-out clothes upon arriving in town, the young man is now dressed in hand-me-down wardrobe a few sizes too big. Jules wears a cartridge belt strapped around his middle, with a fancily-engraved six-shooter perched on his hip.

Just a few steps behind the Texas Rangers, Jules utters, "Excuse me, Ranger Bentley... Hobbs?"

The two men stop and turn around. The taller ranger, Bentley, has a clear eye about him, but Ranger Hobbs staggers, attempting to hold himself up, and appears deep in his cups. Ranger Bentley looks at the boy and replies, "Mister Ward."

Jules stands before them and pushes back his hat. Several pedestrians on the sidewalk move around them, while a mangy-looking dog that follows at the boy's heels keeps a vigilant watch. The boy looks to Bentley and clears his throat before speaking. "Sir... I was wondering when would be the next time you were going to be out searching for outlaws?"

Amused by the mention of outlaws, Hobbs cracks a grin at Bentley, and then peers curiously at the scruffy dog. He looks at the holster rig that hangs around the boy's waist and the fancy shooter that sticks out from the oversized coat. He gestures drunkenly at the boy. "Jules, what is that you got tucked b'hind yer sleeve?"

The boy self-consciously adjusts the six-shooter on his hip and pulls the big coat over it, as he looks back to Bentley. "I would like to accompany you on your next outing."

The ranger looks down at the young man and shakes his head. "I'm afraid we can't take you with us unless you were hired on as a Texas Ranger." Bentley feels compassion for the orphaned youth, but doesn't see another option.

With an intoxicated smirk, Hobbs casually reaches out and pulls the lapel of Jules coat away to get a closer look at the ivory-handled gun holstered on the boy's hip. "I'll be damned. This kid is ready for some fightin' action!"

Jules jerks his coat away from Hobbs' grasp, stands to his full height and looks up at the pair of Texas Rangers. "What does it take to join up?"

Ranger Hobbs stumbles over to lean on a porch support post, as Ranger Bentley shakes his head at the boy before them. "I'm afraid it's not that simple. Most rangers are hired on in an as-needed basis. A small group of us will be traveling the rounds tomorrow, but we're all full up on men."

Letting out a soft whistle, Ranger Hobbs rests the palm of his hand on his own holstered gun. He glances at the dog nested in the dirt beside the sidewalk and then back at Jules. "Any kid game enough to be carrying a fancy six-shooter like that around town is all right in my book. And, that-there dog. Heaven help the poor fella that gits in his way!"

Above the Llano

Jules keeps his attention on Ranger Bentley, replying, "You'll need someone to tend to the men's horses or to help make meals for you. I can work."

Ranger Bentley smiles and nods. "Each man does that for himself, and there ain't no money for extra."

"You won't even have to pay me. Just a scrap of food here and there, and I'd be happy to help, best I can."

Bentley shakes his head at Jules, and the ranger beside him draws a gold coin out of his pocket and flips it to the boy. "If ya bring that ugly, Indian-sniffin' dog with you, yer hired." The boy catches the coin, looks at it and then back up at Ranger Hobbs. "Are you serious?"

Bentley turns to his partner with a dour expression. "Are you serious…?"

Hobbs pushes off the porch support, stands straight, and does his best to keep his wobbly feet underneath him. "I've got that new saddle mount that needs extra tendin', and I sure don't like when it gets to be my turn to cook."

Bentley shakes his head at his partner and grumbles. "He can't come along."

Hobbs reaches out to the porch post for support again and pulls his shoulders back. "Why not?" He waves a hand at Dog, who lifts an ear. "Hell, that mean ol' dog of his is worth more'n the other greenies we're ridin' with."

The two rangers stand quietly for a moment, as Bentley thinks on the proposition. Jules waits and watches them both, expecting more words of protest. Finally, Bentley looks to his ranger partner and grunts. "You are drunk."

Hobbs grins and winks at Jules. "Yep, and tomorrow, I'll be some sober with a fine young feller to tend to my horse, and you'll be the same old, crusty ranger as before." Obviously displeased with the arrangement, Ranger Bentley remains quiet.

Excited, Jules looks over at Dog before tucking the coin in his vest pocket. He respectfully peers up at Ranger Bentley and states, "I don't want to be where I'm not wanted, so if you are still in the mind to not have me along, I won't."

With a sigh, the big Texas Ranger nods. "Mister Ward, you're welcome to come along, but…" Bentley tilts his head to look down at the fancy pistol tucked just inside Jules' coat. "I'd appreciate it if you'd leave the shooting of outlaws to us."

With a serious expression, Jules returns the nod. "Yes… I can do that, save one."

Bentley queries… "Bloody Ben?"

"Yes, sir."

"Fair 'nough."

Slapping his thigh, Hobbs laughs at the tenacity of the young boy. He turns to step away and partly trips on his large roweled spurs. "Dammit! I got to remember to kick these off when I come to town…" He looks back at Jules and salutes. "See ya tomorrow kid."

Bentley adds, "We leave at daybreak."

The youth can't help but let a smile cross his features. He watches the Texas Rangers continue down the sidewalk. Covering the fancy pistol handle with his coat, Jules crosses the street and makes his way to the livery. Dog stands, shakes off the dust from the road, and follows.

Chapter 5

In the northern part of Arizona Territory, Holton rides along a tree-lined path leading to the higher elevations near Prescott. His gaze turns upward to the blue sky, and he breathes deeply the cooling breeze that sways the fringe of his buckskin shirt. Sensing the comfort of being so close to his old home range, he prods his horse to step a little livelier.

The crisp mountain air brings the scent of fresh pine to Holton's nostrils. His calm is broken by the muffled pop of a gunshot reverberating in the far distance. Halting his horse, Holton watches the animal perk its ears to the faraway sound. All is quiet, until the drifting wind carries several more faint sounds of gunfire.

The leather-clad Westerner looks down to where the dog would usually be standing on alert beside his mount. Annoyed, he shakes his head with the recurrent reminder. "No use looking for you, Dog, if you're not gonna be around." With a grimace, he chides himself for talking aloud and prods his horse onward at a loping trot toward the distant gunfire.

~*~

Approaching the ranch homestead formerly owned by his pal, Charlie Nichols, a look of concern comes over Holton.

The gunfire ceases momentarily, but he realizes that the shots were coming from near the supposedly uninhabited cabin. Looking eastward, Holton calculates the nearest neighbors are probably more than a few miles away.

As the sun sets lower on the horizon, Holton quickens his pace and softly mutters, "Don't suspect anyone should be shooting up the Nichols' place since there ain't anyone there." Ahead down the overgrown trail, he sees the arching ranch gate of the vacant spread. Holton keeps to the side of the trail, readying himself for any surprises. He narrows his eyes toward the cabin, and then the outbuildings, and murmurs, "Almost home. Wonder who came to visit...?"

~*~

Holton proceeds through the gate and down the unkempt lane toward the seemingly unoccupied dwellings. As he rides nearer, he notices several horses in the corral and a canvas-covered supply wagon parked alongside the old barn. One of the animals in the corral looks vaguely familiar, and Holton searches his memory for the identity of the owner. Before he can announce himself, a rifle shot rings out from the surrounding rocks.

Tumbling from the saddle, Holton hits the ground with a thump and rolls to the cover of the scrub alongside the trail. Several more shots ring out, and Holton can hear the whizzing of bullet lead crashing through the underbrush nearby. Keeping still, he glances at the bloody tear at the shoulder seam of his buckskin shirt.

Being careful not to reveal his hidden position by shifting around too much, Holton peers through the bushes. He watches his saddled mount amble forward a few steps, stop, then lower its head to begin to graze at a patch of grass. Looking up to the rocky hillside surrounding the ranch, Holton tries to make out who the multiple shooters might be.

Catching a glimpse of someone moving to another position, Holton murmurs. "Damn squatters, I suppose…"

Another set of rifle shots comes from someone hidden in the high rocks. Holton's attention is turned toward the cabin, as an answering gunshot is returned from the window. He shifts slightly to get a better vantage and sees several more flashes of gunfire coming from the shaded interior. Wincing at the nagging pain from his shoulder wound, he groans. "Hmm… What's going on in there?"

The light of evening begins to fade, as the sun dips lower behind the rocky horizon to the west. Concealed in the brush, Holton carefully reaches over to touch where the bullet cut through his shirt and grazed his skin. The wound throbs with a burning sensation, but the bleeding has stopped.

Shifting onto his side, he looks back to the cabin again. Then he surveys the surrounding terrain. Several times he thinks he can see a hint of movement, but he can't make out who or how many might be up there. Their locations are betrayed by the occasional shimmer of evening light reflected off their weapons. Holton looks again to his horse as it stands near the trail with its hind leg cocked, head down, sleeping. With slow, deliberate breaths to take his mind off the pain at his shoulder, Holton closes his eyes and waits for darkness.

~*~

As night falls, Holton lies still in the scrub brush at the edge of the untended road. Sensing that it might be dark enough to hide his movements, he creeps through the brush and makes his way to his horse. Moving slowly and silently, Holton keeps to the edge of the lane and the cover of vegetation. A few feet from his horse, Holton stops to listen. His eyes peer up to his rifle tucked in the leather scabbard hanging alongside the saddle. Cautious, he considers his chances at making a grab for it. He slowly rises to a squatted position, all the while attentive to any nearby sounds.

Straining his eyes to the night, Holton notes the moon is starting to rise, casting illumination on the nearby hills. Determining that his best chance is probably before the moonlight brightens up the valley, he rises to his feet and steps up to his horse. As he reaches over the saddle and puts his hand on the stock of his rifle, the sound of a hammer clicking back on a firearm is heard, breaking the dark stillness.

Chapter 6

"Hold it right there, fella!"

Standing beside his horse with his arm over the saddle, Holton stops. He turns his head in the direction of the voice and squints into the dark. Trying to determine the distance, Holton replies, "Who is that?"

"I could be askin' the same thing." There is a soft rustling in the bushes, as the man steps onto the trail.

"The name is Holton Lang. I own this here spread." Holton quickly scans through the darkness trying to pinpoint the man's exact position.

"Holton Lang, ya say?"

"That's right."

"That old cavalry scout and dispatch rider?"

"The same."

"I heard you were gone… dead somewheres in Texas."

Holton gets a better idea of the man's position off his flank and replies, "I guess you heard wrong."

When the conversation pauses, Holton listens intently. He hears the man's boots shuffle on the gravel trail at the edge of the brush. The footsteps come nearer and Holton queries, "And who might you be?"

"We own this place now."

Pressed up against his horse, Holton remains motionless with his hand still on the big-loop rifle in the scabbard. Holton has a fairly good notion where the man is, but it is still too dark to see anything clearly. He wraps his fingers tighter around the gun stock and prudently observes, "I don't remember selling it."

The man stops advancing, plants his feet and grumbles, "Squatters rights is what we got."

Turning his head further, Holton squints through the dim light and can barely make out the figure in the roadway. "If you're out here, then who is that inside the cabin?"

Following a long, uneasy pause, the man coughs to clear something from his throat. After his bout of coughing, the man speaks with a raspy voice. "You jest step away from that horse, Lang... Slow and careful..."

The moonlight is steadily spreading down the hillside toward them, and Holton figures on it reaching them soon. Slowly, he takes a step back from his mount, but, as he does, he starts to pull the rifle up and out from the saddle scabbard. Directing his voice toward the man, Holton remarks casually, "I take it the ones inside ain't friendly toward you?"

"I said step back from that horse, or I'll shoot you!"

Staring in the direction of the man, Holton takes the chance that the unfriendly squatters can't see him any better than he can see them. In a swift movement, he tugs the rifle from the scabbard and leaps away. The bright flash from a rifle muzzle erupts from the darkness followed by the sound of boots scuffling into the brush. Holton dashes the other way, as another gunshot explodes into the night. He levers his rifle and returns fire, but the sound of the bullet smashing against the rocks tells of a missed shot.

Making his way through the darkness, Holton blinks his eyes to erase the blind-spot created by the blinding flash.

Above the Llano

Staying low as he runs toward the cabin, he uses any obstacle he can find to keep from being silhouetted and becoming an easy target. Stopping at the supply wagon, Holton looks it over and recognizes the rig. Astounded, he utters, "Bear…?"

Against the night sky, Holton sees a trickle of wood smoke coming from the chimney. He smells the aroma of a cooked meal in the air and looks to the dark cabin windows to see the faint glint of a rifle barrel inside. Slipping around the wagon to get a bit closer, Holton hisses a loud whisper. "Bear… Is that you inside?"

A gunshot rings out and smashes into the sideboard of the wooden wagon, just above Holton's head. He drops to the ground and quietly crawls forward under the wagon's tongue. Keeping low, Holton strains his eyes into the night shadows. When there is noticeable movement inside the cabin window, he calls out again. "Bear…! It's me, Holton."

A familiar, booming voice calls out from the cabin. "Holton Lang! You ol' Jack a' nape! Whatcha doin' out there?"

"I ain't come just for your cookin'!"

Holton slinks along the ground, making his way toward the cabin, keeping to the shadows. When he finally makes his way up onto the porch, several gunshots blast out from the surrounding rocks. Holton gives a holler, as he dives for the front door. "Open up, Bear! I'm comin' in!"

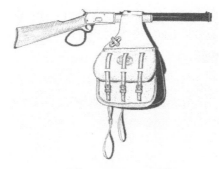

Chapter 7

The front door of the cabin swings open just as Holton dives through. He is followed by several rounds of bullets that smash into the wooden threshold. Holton tumbles across the plank floor toward the smoldering fireplace, and the door is quickly slammed shut behind him. Clutching his rifle across his chest, he sits up in the glowing light of the cook fire and hears his old friend's voice in the dimness. "Dang, Holton... Missy, light that candle to have a look-see what we got here."

A matchstick is struck against the rough-hewn surface of the table, and the glowing tip is put to a wick of a candle. The room lights up to show Holton, seated on the floor, looking up at Bear and then over toward Alice Weathersby. Shocked, yet relieved at the same time, Holton stares at the woman who was the former captive of Bloody-Ben Sighold. "Alice?" Confused, Holton looks back to Bear. "What the hell is she doing here?"

Alice crinkles her brow and then blows out the match. She pushes the candle holder across the table, as Holton climbs to his feet. "Mister Lang, I can speak for myself."

Dumbfounded, Holton regards the woman, uttering, "Okay, Ma'am, then speak. How was it you ended up here?" Mouth agape, he stares at her and waits for an answer.

With the light from the candle twinkling in her eyes, Alice returns Holton's blank stare. "Mister Benton here was kind enough to let me accompany him to his ranch instead of deserting me in town."

When Holton turns to look at Bear, his friend nearly swallows his chewing tobacco before sheepishly replying, "She's a hard woman to be rid of."

With the question of the ranch's ownership lingering, Holton inquires, "His ranch, is it?"

Bear leans over to spit into the fire and wipes his lips. "Well, we didn't go over the specific details."

Holton holds his rifle across his middle and notices the blanket-covered windows, clutter, and the general disrepair of the cabin. "That's the second time today I've heard folks claim ownership of this place."

In the light of the candle, Alice sweeps some crumbs from the tabletop into her cupped hand. She peers up at Holton and states, "The point is that I wasn't to be left in town to the ridicule of society."

Holton watches her toss the crumbs into the fireplace before he mutters. "But, you don't belong here."

"Where do I belong, Mister Lang?"

He turns to Bear, as the old military scout hooks a finger inside his full cheek, scoops, and tosses away his chaw. He then looks to the head-strong woman standing before him. The three stand in the room staring at each other curiously.

After no one speaks, Holton finally shakes his head in frustration and goes to the window to peek out. A gunshot blasts from the darkness and crashes through the opening.

Above the Llano

Holton lets the curtain fall closed again and turns to Bear. "Who is that out there shooting?

Taking up a chair by the stone fireplace, Bear grabs his smoking pipe off the mantle. He inspects the loosely-packed tobacco in the bowl then reaches over to the table and holds it over the candle flame to light it. Glancing across the room at Holton, he replies, "They was here already when we arrived, and that was more'n a week ago."

Holton watches Bear take a puff from the pipe and sees the smoke filter through the silver whiskers around his lips. Bear takes the pipe from his mouth, licks the front of his teeth, and then clenches the stout clay stem in his jaw as he speaks. "We tried to explain to them 'bout ownership of this here property, but they run us off for our efforts."

Looking around the cluttered cabin, Holton takes note of the personal belongings of its former resident. The interior remains pretty much the way it was when Charlie last occupied it. He looks to Alice again and then back at Bear. "How'd you finally take up in here?"

Bear puffs on his pipe and tips the stem toward Alice. "I was ready to give it up and move on, but Alice here is a tough woman to discourage. She had us stake out a camp on the hill 'til most of them damn squatters were out and about. Then, we come down here and took proper possession."

Holton snorts and heaves a heavy sigh. "So, now you're trapped in here?" Bear merely shrugs as he smokes his pipe. "All depends on how you look at it. We got their supply of grub in here... So, could be that they're stuck out there!"

Picking up a rifle, Alice moves to stand near the door. "And what would you have us do?" Her eyes flicker with determination, as she looks across the room at the two men. "When something is taken away, you do your damnedest to get it back and make it right."

Holton exchanges a solemn look with Alice and then turns to Bear again. "You were supposed to deliver her safely to Santa Fe and leave it at that."

From behind him, Alice clears her throat and sternly proclaims, "Mister Lang, I am safest behind this loaded rifle, and I don't appreciate you dictating where I should and shouldn't be left off." A puff of smoke drifts from Bear's pipe as he grunts, "She's a hard woman to quit."

Holton glances over to where Bear smokes contentedly and grumbles at him. "You mentioned that already."

Alice turns to hide her smile and then peeks outside. From the moonlit hills, a rifle shot sends a bullet through the window covering and smashes low into the opposite wall. Bear gestures to the candle. "We'd best snuff out that light, now that we know who is who."

Holton leans over the table to blow out the flame, and the room falls back into darkness.

Chapter 8

The only illumination in the cabin comes from the soft glow of embers in the fireplace. Listening for sounds of the men outside, they only hear a hooting call of an owl near the barn. Holton moves across the dark room and draws the curtain aside just enough to see into the brighter moonlight outside. "How many are out there?"

The bowl of Bear's pipe glows bright, and he mutters, "There was five of 'em initially."

Holton looks back toward the fireplace and can barely make out Bear's bearded features in the dim light of the fire. "How many out there now?"

"Well... She put one of 'em out of business for good." The scout glances at Alice and then looks back toward Holton. "We let 'em drag the body away awhile 'fore you arrived."

"Who are they?"

"Squatters from Missouri is as far as we got with introductions." Bear rocks back in the chair and stretches. "There weren't much of a social gathering on the subject."

Alice stands in the shadows by the doorway, holding the rifle. She grunts and comments, "They're like locusts moving west. Taking up what they can..."

As he glances to her, Holton lets the curtain fall closed. "They ain't gonna be too keen to move on anytime soon, since they lost one of theirs at this place."

Alice sweeps back her hair and is unremorseful in her reply. "They wasn't too keen to move on regardless."

"How was it you both came to be in here again?"

Bear taps the bowl of his pipe on his palm and grins. "Like I said, most of 'em was out and about, and we come down to have us another visit. One of 'em come out a-shootin' at us, and she returned the unfriendly gesture." He puffs on the glowing bud of tobacco in his pipe, blows out a cloud of smoke and snorts. "One damn shot and that fella hit the dirt, deader'n a post."

Alice opens the door a bit, peers out into the moonlight, and her womanly features are momentarily illuminated. Pulling back, she lets her gaze travel to Holton and then back to Bear. "There's no need to waste lead on that sort of trash."

Bear nods his approval. "No, ma'am, you did not."

Holton watches her close the door to a crack and asks, "What was your plan after that?"

Bear coughs out a bit of pipe smoke before replying. "You're looking at it now, Holton. We jest plan to wait here 'til they go away."

"They sure don't seem all that discouraged…"

Holding the rifle, Alice peeks out the doorway again. "They might be, after we put a few more in the ground."

Pointing the clay stem of his pipe at her, Bear chuckles. "She done winged another one of 'em, but he ain't dead."

Alice puts the rifle to her shoulder, sights down the barrel and murmurs, "Not yet…"

Stepping away into the shadows, Holton takes a deep breath and winces at his bullet-grazed shoulder wound.

"Well, I'm gonna get some rest, and we can mull over what to do in the light of morning."

Bear spits aside into the smoldering fire and comments, "That's as good a plan as any."

Keeping the rifle barrel pointed out through the door, Alice quietly whispers, "I'll keep watch."

Holton turns to look at Bear seated by the fireplace. "She been taking okay care of you?" The rickety chair Bear sits in creaks, as he leans back. He nods while continuing to enjoy smoking his pipe. "Yup… She's bin doin' a fine job."

~*~

The morning sun begins to crest over the surrounding hills, and a new day shines on the isolated ranch buildings. There is a hint of movement a good distance from the cabin, as one of the squatters rushes over to join another. Bear grumbles over his shoulder, after he takes a peek out the window. "They's up and movin' now."

Stirring a pot of breakfast, Alice stands by the fireplace. Her attention moves to Holton, who lies on a blanket spread out on the floor. He stirs awake and lifts up on an elbow. "They near enough to get a shot off?"

"Not for me, it ain't. If we had that sharpshooter along, Private Dedman, it would be good-night-ladies for all of 'em out there."

Holton grimaces, looks around the cabin and comments sarcastically. "I'm surprised he's not here with you along with a passel of other folks."

Bear leans back from the window and grins. "Heck, for being such a lonesome fella, ya sure do attract a crowd."

"I come here alone."

Bear chuckles. "And now look at ya…"

Frustrated with his old pal, Holton turns his thoughts to sustenance when he smells what Alice has in the cook pot.

He turns to face her, and notices that she has been keenly watching him. "Morning, ma'am."

"It's Alice."

"I know."

Looking to his torn leather shirt and blood-crusted shoulder wound, she sets aside her task of preparing the meal. "Would you like me to tend to your shoulder?"

He peers down at the flesh wound and tilts his head. "It ain't bleeding none now."

"It should be cleaned."

Holton glimpses over toward Bear, who merely grins. He shakes his head at Alice and grabs up his rifle before moving to the window to look out. "I will tend to it later."

Bear moves the curtain aside and takes another gander. "Yaugh, it's probably better to mend all the battle wounds at one time, after the fightin' is over."

Holton grimaces at Bear, looks to Alice and then turns his focus outside. "Where they at?"

Bear mutters, "Jest past the creek, up by them rocks."

Alice adds, "Same as yesterday."

"It's a good position." Careful not to become a target, Holton sneaks a peek outside and spots a bit of movement on the hillside across the way. He moves back to the interior of the cabin and sits at the table. "They'll hold out there until we give 'em somethin' to shoot at."

Bear grunts dismissively. "Ya don't think they'll get bored and go on home?"

"Back to Missouri?"

Alice mutters under her breath. "Probably not welcome there, either."

Bear watches her bring the pot of breakfast to the table and put a plate before Holton. "Yer prob'ly right 'bout that. It's not very likely."

Above the Llano

Holton looks across the room at Bear. "After breakfast, I'll sneak up there, and see what I kin do."

Stomach growling at the smell of the morning meal, Bear notices Alice purposefully ladle servings onto Holton's plate, again and again, until he acknowledges her with a halting look. The scout giggles and adds, "Sounds good, pard. I'll go along with ya."

The buckskin-clad westerner looks down to his overfilled plate and then over to the former military scout. "No. I'll need you to keep their attention while I slip away."

"What? Like some kinda bait?"

With a smile, Holton nods. "Something like that."

Propping his rifle against the window sill, Bear comes to the table for his meal. "They ain't bin very good shots so far, but I'd hate fer my rockin' chair out front to get torn up." Alice hands Bear a plate of food that has only a small portion compared to what she served Holton. He looks at the meager serving and then to the chair. "Cain't I even set down?"

She ushers him back to the window and proclaims, "You need to be on lookout, so they don't stroll on in here." The seasoned scout glances to his underserved ration of food again and whines, "Do I at least get another helpin'?"

In a reprimanding fashion, Alice gives Bear a spirited shove back toward the front window where his rifle rests. "Bear, you know too much grub will make you sleepy."

Holton takes up his fork and scoops a mouthful. Chewing, he wisely states, "Yes, Bear... It's not the minutes that make you portly..." He swallows. "It's the seconds."

The old scout looks dour, as he returns to guard duty by the window again, and starts to eat while standing upright. He gazes toward Holton, grumbling, "I was taken care of a lot better before you showed up..."

Chapter 9

The front door of the cabin opens, and Bear cautiously steps outside onto the covered porch. He casts his gaze all around while carrying his rifle held high against his chest. Keeping to the shade of the porch, he hollers, "Listen here, ya home-poachin' sons-of-a-gun! Come on down, and we'll talk some about this here situation." Out of the corner of his eye, he sees Holton crawling through a hole in the rock-stacked foundation beneath the cabin. When Holton, rifle in hand, makes his way to the corral, Bear looks up to the hillside, lowers the gun from across his chest and hollers, "Ya hear me out there...?"

Across the way, two men with rifles step from the concealment of the rocks. They look at Holton's saddled mount as it grazes peacefully nearby, and call out to Bear. "Who's that Indian-lookin' feller in there with you?"

Not wanting to let on as he watches Holton making his way along the fence line, Bear calls back to the two squatters. "That be Holton Lang, the proper owner of this here spread." The foremost squatter looks at his partner and remarks, "T'ain't so... He's dead."

Bear takes another step forward on the porch, stopping with his toe at the dark line of shadow from the overhang.

"There's been many that tried to kill him o'er the years, but they ain't got the job done yet."

Unsure, the squatters look at each other, and briefly converse before one of them tips his hat and hollers back. "Tell 'im to step out here, so we can have a closer look at 'im."

As Bear pivots toward the cabin door, he catches a glimpse of Holton slipping around to the back of the barn. Peering inside the cabin, he calls through the doorway. "Holton... Why don't you come out to the porch here and show yerself?" In the shadowed entry, someone pokes a rifle barrel out and then appears.

Bear stares at Alice, outfitted in a pair of men's britches, drop-sleeved shirt, and a cowboy hat pulled low on her head. Trying to keep from smiling, Bear rubs a hand over his mouth, clears his throat and turns to address the pair of squatters. "You fellas hear me alright up there?" The squatters keep their rifles at the ready, as they step forward to see the porch better. Bear hollers out to them. "That's near 'nough, I reckon. Holton here ain't too keen on bein' shot at or havin' to fight his way back home." He glances back at Alice before he continues. "He says for you all to move along down the trail, 'fore he gets real angry and someone else gits hurt or killed."

Still too far away to see into the porch shadows clearly, the squatters squint their eyes trying to make out the figure in the doorway. One of the squatters pushes his hat way back on his head, puts his hand to his brow and shades his eyes. Finally, he orders, "The both of yous... Step out into the sun!"

Bear keeps to his position at the edge of the shadows and shakes his bearded chin. "No-siree... We ain't coming out any further, until the rest of you pot-shot-takin' homestead-jumpers show yerselves first." He keeps his rifle ready and glances behind at Alice again.

Above the Llano

The two squatters exchange a suspicious stare, and one of them shakes his head. Disingenuously, the other replies, "They already gone without us. Step out here, and we'll talk."

Bear takes a few steps back from the forward edge of the porch, as he senses the sights of a rifle aimed on him. Keeping the cocked rifle held across his chest, he shouts, "When y'all git where we can see ya, we'll come out."

One of the squatters makes a waving motion with his arm and a third man steps out from the adjacent rocks. Carrying a shotgun, the man makes his way to the others. The leader of the group turns to Bear and grins. "There ya go. Now you both come out to where we can see ya clear."

His rifle held ready, Bear remains standing mid-porch. Unsure, he eyes the three men carefully and shakes his head. "There was five of ya yesterday."

"You done killed our cousin…"

"What about the other one?"

"Him, too!"

The squatter coming down from the rocks casually looks past his shoulder and touches the brim of his hat in a subtle signaling gesture. Suddenly, a rifle shot explodes from a hiding spot amongst the rocks, and the blast splinters a chunk of the porch between Bear's feet. From beside the barn, a second rifle shot toward the rocks quickly follows.

Raising his rifle and putting it to his shoulder, Bear jumps back to cover Alice at the doorway. He scans the gun sights past the men in front of the cabin and up to the rock outcroppings beyond. One of the squatters turns and yells to the man in the rocks. "Ya missed 'im, ya dunderhead!!!"

Holton stands up from his hiding place and levers a fresh round into the chamber. He calls out to the squatters. "He missed, I didn't…"

The three men's first reaction is to scatter for cover. Holton fires a round into the upper thigh of one of them, dropping him to the ground and slowing up the two others. Bear rushes forward, jumps off the porch and points his rifle. "Hold it where you are fellas, or we'll finish the job!"

The two squatters stand over their wounded kinfolk, glaring daggers at Bear. The most talkative one grumbles, "That's some damned dishonest work you done to us."

A grin breaks through Bear's beard, and he replies, "That's the kinda treatment squatters git 'round these parts. Now toss away them shootin' irons."

The three hold tight to their firearms, looking around and considering their odds. They watch, as Holton makes his way over from the barn, and Bear glances back at Alice in the cabin doorway with a rifle held on them all. The man with the wounded leg whimpers, "What're you gonna do with us?"

Keeping his rifle pointed directly at the talkative one, a stern expression comes over Bear's features. "We'll deliver you to the military camp, or maybe the law o'er in Prescott."

Looking hard and determined, even under the focus of the pointed rifles, the lead squatter looks aside and spits. Finally, he gruffly replies, "Naw, we cain't do that."

Looking at the man down his rifle sights, Bear asks, "Why not?"

"Cause we done and killed several folks hereabouts, and I don't intend to hang fer it."

Chapter 10

Curious to the man's meaning, Bear lowers his aim slightly. "And who might that be?"

The squatter gives a noticeable nudge to his partner, and the other man wraps his hand tighter around the forestock of his Sharps rifle. The leader glances over at Holton coming from the barn and then faces back to Bear, replying, "You all…!"

The man quickly lifts his rifle and fires a shot at Bear, which rips into the fleshy part of the scout's abdomen. Doubled over, Bear stumbles backward and fires off his rifle. The blast smashes into the forehead of the man standing next to the shooter, and he drops to the ground, dead.

The leg-wounded squatter on the ground raises his shotgun to shoot, and Alice fires from the cabin doorway, hitting him dead-center with a bullet to the chest. With all his compatriots gunned down around him, the last man standing fires his rifle toward the cabin. As he levers the action on his gun, he turns to see Holton approaching.

Hopping over a cluster of rocks, Holton fires his rifle at the same time the squatter fires. The dueling clouds of black powder smoke envelope the pair of shooters momentarily before drifting away.

His feet planted, Holton cocks the lever action of his big-loop rifle, ejecting the empty shell and loading another. His opponent stares vacantly at him, standing motionless as the tip of his rifle barrel trickles smoke. Moving a step closer, Holton takes stock and quickly ascertains that he doesn't have any newly acquired injuries.

The man opposite Holton has a bullet hole through his throat, just above his collar. He coughs and a gurgle of blood erupts from the gaping wound. "You really are Holton Lang... Damn it all..." When the man tumbles forward over his rifle, Holton turns to see Bear laying on the ground.

Alice rushes from the cabin doorway to Bear's side and then looks to Holton standing amongst the three shot-down squatters. She lifts Bear's head and gingerly inspects the bleeding bullet wound in his midsection. A foreboding of loss sweeps over Holton, and he clenches his jaw to hold back his emotions. The squatter with the hole through his neck gurgles faintly and starts to roll over. "Help me... I ain't dead."

Kneeling on the ground, Alice, holding Bear's limp body, looks up at Holton. Breathless, she gasps, "Are you going to take care of him?!?" Holton looks into the pleading man's eyes and then over to his gut-shot friend on the ground. Without hesitation, he lifts the barrel of the rifle and aims it at the man's head. The squatter clasps the bloody hole in his neck, gurgling in protest as Holton pulls the trigger and sends a bullet through his brain.

Alice dispassionately witnesses the mercy killing. Holton steps away from the three lifeless men, looks to the woman cradling his friend in her arms and faintly inquires, "Is he dead?"

She looks up at him and then shakes her head slightly. "No, but it's a bad wound."

Above the Llano

Holton slowly uncocks his rifle, drops it to the ground, and kneels down next to Bear. He attempts to scoop his friend up in his arms, strains with the bulkier man's weight and finally gets a hold of him under the arms. Alice remains kneeling, as Holton drags the scout to the cabin, up the stairs, and in through the front door. She looks down at the special big-loop rifle discarded in the dirt, picks it up and stands. Between the slain squatters and the cabin, Alice cradles Holton's rifle in her arms and casts her gaze around the now quiet ranch compound.

~*~

There is a crusted pool of dried blood in the dirt near three sets of heel-drag marks. The parallel trails lead to a shallow, unmarked grave at the edge of the scrub brush. Holton shovels a final layer of dirt over the bodies.

Alice steps out from the cabin doorway, hesitating briefly on the porch stoop before walking over toward Holton. She watches him toss a few handfuls of large rocks over the mounded bodies to discourage critters from digging at them. As she approaches, he stops and turns to look at her. Anxiously wiping her hands together, Alice looks at the mounds and inquires, "Are all five of them in there?"

"Jest the three of 'em. The coyotes got to the one up in the rocks and scattered him all around." He wipes the sweat from his brow and adjusts his hat. "I couldn't find the one you shot 'fore I arrived the other day."

Alice instinctively looks up and around to the surrounding hills. "He won't be bothering us from hell."

"You sure of that?"

Without the least bit of regret, the frontier-weary female turns back to look at Holton and states, "Pretty sure that's the place where I sent 'im."

Satisfied with her estimation, Holton nods and leans on the short-handled shovel stuck in the ground beside him. They both stare at the mound of freshly buried bodies, and he murmurs, "How is Bear?"

"He's alive yet, for now."

Not finding the appropriate words to express himself, there is a long pause until Holton finally utters, "Thank you."

She looks at him questioningly. "What for?"

"For all that you done for me 'n Bear... and the boy."

Alice nods appreciative and turns away. Looking back, she regards him momentarily, about to say something. Thinking better of it, she continues to stroll back to the cabin. Clenching his jaw, Holton glances over his shoulder to watch her go. Then, he pulls up the shovel, pats it on the grave, and makes his way to the barn.

Chapter 11

The late afternoon sunlight shining through the windows of the cabin intensifies just before setting behind the rocky hills. Seated next to the stone fireplace, Holton holds a clay smoking pipe in hand. He looks to the bunk of the former owner, Charlie Nichols, where his longtime friend, Bear, is sleeping with short, shallow breaths.

Alice comes in from sitting on the porch and looks to Holton by the hearth. She has a nagging question on her mind but is reluctant to speak about it. Fleetingly meeting her gaze, Holton watches as she moves to the wounded man in the bed to check on his condition. Bear moans, as she sweeps back the sweated hair from his forehead and tests him for fever.

Leaning forward, Holton gives a tap of Bear's pipe on his open palm. "How long will you stay?"

Startled by the candid inquiry, Alice straightens up and turns to face Holton. "Why, Mister Lang... I was going to ask you the same thing."

He stands to place Bear's pipe back on the fireplace mantle and then looks down to the crackling flames. "I really have no place in particular that I'm needed."

Smoothing her skirt, Alice takes a seat at Bear's bedside and watches Holton stare into the fire. Finally, she offers, "You're needed here."

He looks over at her for a moment then he turns away. "I don't know what I can do for him…"

Alice lowers her gaze and rests her hand on the torso of the wounded man on the bunk. She feels his chest rise, lungs filling with shallow breath, and then looks back up at Holton. "There is nothing else to be done for now. The bullet passed through without hitting any vitals, and he will heal or not."

Holton bites his lip and murmurs under his breath. "Sure hate not knowing…"

Painfully, he rolls his injured shoulder back, and Alice frowns as she notices again the crusting of blood on his buckskin shirt. "Will you let me tend to that wound of yours?"

Holton peers down at his bullet-creased shoulder where his leather shirt is stuck to the scabbed wound and winces as he pulls it away. He crosses the room to the doorway, grabbing his rifle before making his way outside. "Maybe later…"

Alice watches Holton head out and calls after him. "Sooner is better than later." He stops a moment on the porch, looks through the front window to her at Bear's bedside, then turns away and steps into the twilight. Alice watches him through the cabin window, until he withdraws into the barn. She lights an oil lamp near her patient's bunk and starts to redress the bloody bandage around his midsection.

~*~

A small group of Texas Rangers rides up to a rural farmstead, which has a German-style log house backed by a cut-stone barn and stables. The riders approach warily, as there are no apparent inhabitants or livestock present.

Above the Llano

Cautious voices murmur, as the riders pass over several distinct sets of unshod pony tracks.

Bringing up the rear, with a pack mule in tow, Jules puts his hand to the handle of his fancy-engraved revolver. The smell of death fills his nostrils, and he remembers back to the dead outlaw who owned the same pistol, months prior. He looks to the front of the group where Ranger Bentley holds up his hand and motions for them to stop a short distance from the seemingly abandoned homestead.

"Hold up boys..."

Disheartened, Ranger Hobbs rides forward and sighs. He puts an elbow to his saddle horn, looks around and comments to Bentley. "Looks to be a bunch of Comanche."

"Could be."

Uncomfortable with the stillness, Hobbs continues to scan the plundered farmstead, listening intently, and mutters. "I doubt these folks took all of their livestock with 'em to a picnic at the neighbors'."

With a long face, Ranger Bentley looks aside at Hobbs. "It appears nobody is here."

Hobs grunts, "Yeah, I noticed."

"I mean, there are no apparent homesteader casualties or any signs of looting."

Their gaze travels to the house, and Hobbs verbalizes what they are both thinking. "We ain't been inside yet."

Shortening the rein on his mount, Bentley stares forward as he speaks to Hobbs. "You take a few of the boys and check the barn and outbuildings. I'll see to the house. We'll leave Jules here to watch the mule and our food stores."

Hobbs pivots in the saddle and gestures at two of the rangers to follow him. With a commanding tone, Bentley then speaks to Jules. "Mister Ward, I want you to stay here with that mule. Everyone else, follow along behind me."

Jules opens his mouth to protest, but decides better of it when he receives a stern look from Ranger Bentley. He nods and replies, simply, "Yes, Sir."

As he watches the rangers ride forward, Jules sits tight, following orders.

Chapter 12

At the stone-cut barn, Ranger Hobbs instructs his two rangers to follow him around to the partly-open side door. They disappear from view, as they ride their mounts inside. The farmstead is eerily silent with the exception of the soft footfalls of the ranger horses and an uneasy nicker from one of the mounts.

At the house, Ranger Bentley dismounts in front of the stoop, draws his sidearm, cocks it, and cautiously knocks before pushing open the unlocked door. A few yards distant, Jules sits, waiting. All is quiet, as he watches the rangers behind Bentley dismount and follow him inside.

Suddenly, a frightening war-whoop breaks the silence. Jules turns to face the barn, and watches as a horseback Comanche races from the opened door. A struggling Texas Ranger, held in a choking headlock, is being dragged alongside the running horse. Shouting his warrior challenge, the Indian heads straight toward Jules and the pack mule.

Without thinking twice, Jules pulls his fancy pistol from his holster and thumbs back the hammer. He takes careful aim and waits a measure for the rider to get closer. Finally, he squeezes the trigger and puts a lead bullet right into the open mouth of the screaming Comanche.

Through a cloud of black-powder smoke, Jules sees the Comanche release his grip on the ranger's neck and tumble backward over the rump of the running horse. The warrior hits the ground hard, bouncing twice before rolling to a stop. After dallying the mule's lead rope around the saddle horn, Jules leaps from his mount. Pistol held ready, he rushes to the aid of the Texan.

The Texas Ranger lies on the ground, clutching his wrenched neck. When Jules kneels over him, he gazes upward with awe, at the boyish features that starkly contrast the maturity of the marksmanship just performed. With the smell of burnt gunpowder still lingering in the air, Jules asks. "Mister Kent...You okay there?"

As the disconcerted ranger tries to swallow through his aching neck, tears of pain and fear well up under his eyes. When the tears finally streak down his dirt-smudged cheeks, Jules gives him comforting pats on the shoulder, commenting, "It's okay now... Try to breathe, and you'll be fine."

Ashamed at his display of emotions, Ranger Kent turns to hide his face from Jules. Understanding, the boy nods his head and whispers to him. "They are all still a ways off... Take some time to compose yerself." Looking back to the barn, Jules sees Ranger Hobbs and the other Texas Ranger exiting on horseback with a native prisoner in tow.

As the rangers' horses graze in front of the house, Ranger Bentley appears in the doorway with two young children clinging tightly to each other. He looks across the yard to Jules kneeling beside Kent, and then turns his gaze to Hobbs and the others, still horseback. With a slight nod and tilt of his head, he looks back to Jules and gestures them all to a clump of shade trees nearby.

~*~

Above the Llano

All the horses are assembled in a picket line, and Jules tends to the unpacking of supplies. He looks to the nearby stand of trees, where the lone Comanche sits with his hands and feet tightly bound. On the ground, in the middle of camp, the children play quietly with a pair of dice provided by one of the Texas Rangers. Jules finishes with the supplies and gear, as Ranger Hobbs walks over to talk with him. "Mister Ward... That was a good shot you took."

Halting his chores, Jules stands up. He stretches as tall as he can, while the Texas Ranger gives him a look-over. "Thank you, Sir."

Hobbs glances at the holstered pistol on the boy's hip. "Normally, we wouldn't be allowin' a youngster like yerself to go packin' iron, let alone, a fancy shooter like that one..." The ranger looks to Jules' saddle with the cloth sack of extra cartridges slung over the horn. "But, Bentley and I talked it over, and you seem to know how to put it to good use."

Jules nods and looks over toward Ranger Bentley who squats down conversing with the noticeably shaken ranger. The boy looks back to Hobbs and asks, "How is he doing?"

"He'll be fine. Probably won't sleep for a few nights, but there's no real damage done on the outside."

"What about them kids?"

"We'll have to get them to a town where someone will find a family for them to stay with."

With a nod, Jules looks away. He can't help getting a swelling of anxiety from the painful memory of his own abducted siblings. He turns back to Ranger Hobbs and utters, "We gonna track down the ones who done this?"

The Texas Ranger turns his contemplation from the camp to Jules. "We're gonna split off a few of us to go to town, and the rest will follow after the marauders."

"I'm going with you."

Eric H. Heisner

"That's what we wanted to talk with you about."

Jules sweeps his gaze across the ranger camp and lets it linger on Bentley. "Who is *we*?"

Sighing, Hobbs replies. "Ranger Bentley and myself…"

Standing up to his full height, Jules instantly protests. "I have fulfilled my end of the arrangement, so I get to come."

"We're pretty sure this is just a renegade group of Comanche, and Bloody Ben is not among them."

Flushing with contempt at the mention of the outlaw, Jules queries, "How would you know that?"

"It just don't seem likely."

Jules stares at Hobbs before looking over to Bentley, who glances in their direction. "I'm going along with you all, whether you like it or not."

The good-humored ranger bows his head and groans. "That's what I told Bentley, but he thought I should try to talk you out of it regardless."

"You ain't."

"Fine. I figured as much. We'll camp here for the night. Tomorrow the company will split ways." As he walks away, Hobbs turns to remark, "Yer lucky you ain't an official ranger, or you'd be ordered one way or t'other, like it or not."

The boy takes a breath and replies, "Yeah, I see that."

Ranger Hobbs is about to say more, but holds back and gives Jules a nodding salute before walking off. Jules looks at the stack of camp supplies, glances to the horses and mule, then looks again to the pair of children playing with the dice.

Chapter 13

Outfitted in a faded, blue military-surplus bib shirt, Holton sits in the rocking chair on the front porch of the ranch cabin. Across his lap, he holds his fringed buckskin shirt and passes a curved sewing needle with animal sinew thread through the shoulder to stitch the bullet-creased tear. Using a thumbnail, he scratches some of the crusted blood from the leather.

Alice steps out from the doorway of the cabin and looks to Holton in the rocker. Cracking a smile, she comments, "Nice to see a man who can sew."

He glances up at her and gives a nod. "I ain't known many who can't."

She retorts, "They seem to forget awful quick when a woman is around to do it."

Holton returns his attention to his sewing and grunts, "How'd you think I made the shirt...?" Feeling reprimanded, Alice bites her tongue and looks out to the view from the cabin's porch. She seems as if she wants to talk with him about something but can't find the right way to bring it up. Noticing her lingering, Holton asks, "How's Bear doing?"

"He's alive yet. Still very weak, but starting to eat."

Holton continues his needlework, tightening the stitch by pulling on the thread. "I'll go out later and hunt us some fresh meat."

"That would be nice to have."

They are quiet for a moment, until Alice finally blurts, "I would like to stay." Holton accidentally pokes himself with the needle and yelps. Alice quickly turns her head and tries to revise her comment. "I mean, as long as Bear needs the attention and help to get better, I'd like to stay."

Sucking on the blood from the needle prick, Holton looks up at her. She stands uncomfortably under his gaze, and he states, "You're welcome to stay here as long as you'd like."

"I just don't want to be thought improper... I don't want to overstep my bounds."

Scanning his gaze around the isolated ranch, Holton fixes his attention on the range of mountains, miles away. "Who is here to say different?"

Smiling nervously at Holton, Alice takes a deep, measured breath to keep up her courage. "Mister Lang... Where I come from, it would be a shameful thing for a woman in my position to take up house with two men like you and Mister Benton."

Holton ties off the thread, puts the needle aside and then shakes out his leather shirt. "Ma'am, where I come from, people do what they want to do and don't take no heed to what others think."

"Where was that? Maybe I would like to go there."

With a laugh, Holton stands and looks over at Alice. "Don't imagine you would like that very much. I lived with the Apache for a good part of my early life."

Quite surprised, Alice doesn't know exactly what to say to him. Holton moves past her, tosses his repaired shirt into the cabin and grabs his rifle from its position by the doorway.

Above the Llano

As he returns back to face Alice, he catches the scent of soap. Modestly, she turns away and replies, "I'm sorry... I didn't know you lived with the Apache."

"There is nothing to be sorry about. It's not something most folks would understand."

Alice moves to the cabin doorway, pauses and stops. "Was it a hard life?"

"It was a good life while it lasted."

She looks longingly at the tall westerner standing before her. "I hear the Apache are cruel."

Not flinching under her scrutiny, Holton nods. "They are fierce fighters, but cruelty comes from all kinds of people. The Spanish taught them many of the harshest lessons, but the whites done their share, too."

At the threshold to the cabin, looking into Holton's eyes, Alice can't decide if she wants to duck away or continue this conversation. "I am a woman alone here with two men of the frontier. Am I safe?"

Holton grins and nods his head. "Yes, ma'am, you're about as safe as can be, west of Missouri. I may be part Indian, some white, and all wild, but I was raised with a respect for woman-folk, and the same goes for our injured friend in there. Treat this homestead as your own, and feel welcome to stay as you wish." The woman clutches the front of her dress, and she glances inside to Bear as he sleeps. Satisfied, she looks back to Holton and nods. "Thank you, Mister Lang."

"You can jest call me Holton from now on, if you please. I'll go and get us that fresh meat for dinner." He turns away, rifle in hand, and walks off the porch toward the barn. Alice stands in the doorway watching him, before quietly stepping back into the shadows.

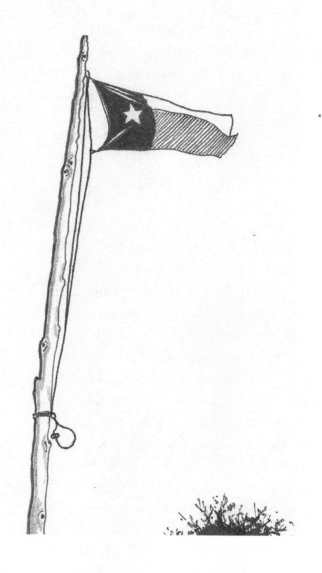

Chapter 14

The Texas Rangers pack their gear and saddle up, preparing to depart the camp near the German farmstead. Jules tends to the animals, while a few of the rangers finish their breakfast. Hands bound and leaned up against a tree, the Comanche captive stares at the group of armed men and small children with a vacant expression on his features.

Finished with tacking his mount, Jules joins the Texans as they discuss their plan for the day. Bentley glances at Kent and then looks to another ranger. "Ranger Hicks, I want you and one other to escort the children and the native to Fredericksburg. We will continue north, on the trail of the marauders, and try to overtake them before they invade the outlying homesteaders."

With a sour look on his face, Ranger Hicks looks around to several of the other Texas Rangers. "Captain... Don't want to be contrary, but I'd like to stay with you and the others to recover any hostages."

Perturbed, Hobbs shakes his head and spits to the side. "Dammit Hicks, you're just wanting to shoot some Indians with that new rifle of yourn. Now, do what you're told!"

Jules notices the increasing tension between the two, as unspoken words ride a sensitive nerve. Ranger Hicks hooks a finger into his mouth and pulls out a wad of chewing tobacco. He slings the wet chaw to the ground, grumbling, "Jest 'cause I ain't the Captain's pet, don't mean I should run escort for an Injun and some kids."

Hobbs peers down at the splash of chew-spit on the toe of his dusty boot and takes a step toward Hicks. "You wipe that spittle off my boot, ya damned dip-slinger!"

Staring at Hobbs, Ranger Hicks takes a defiant stance. "You clean the boots in this camp!" Everyone watches as Hobbs leaps at Hicks, and the two rangers begin to tussle.

Jules steps back and moves next to Ranger Bentley. Noticing him watching the fight, he looks up to the ranger and inquires, "Ain't you gonna stop 'em?"

"Some men need to get that sort of thing off their chest. Sooner is better than later."

"Won't they kill each other?"

"I'll put an end to it b'fore it gets that far."

They watch Hicks climb to his feet and deliver a swinging kick to Hobbs. Everyone cringes as the leather boot connects with a thump, and Ranger Hobbs tumbles backward. When Hicks walks over to the ranger on the ground to see if he needs to finish the job, Hobbs sweeps his arm out and takes the other ranger's feet out from under him.

In a flash, Hobbs is on top and delivers a knockout blow to Hicks' chin. Hand clenched and raised, he is about to deliver another punch when Ranger Bentley steps forward and calls out. "Okay Hobbs, that's enough!"

Taking a breath to calm himself, Ranger Hobbs breaks from his angry rage and holds back. He looks down at Hicks sprawled on the ground and pushes back to stand over him. Hobbs winces at his sore midsection while shaking his head and tugging the front of his vest down. He steps away from

Hicks and bends down to sweep his hat up off the ground. "Yeah... It's all over anyhow."

The crowd of Texans breaks up, and they slowly make their way to their mounts. Hicks props himself up on an elbow and rubs his chin, sluggishly starting to come around. He looks up at Hobbs and then over to Bentley standing nearby. The ranger captain stares at the two of them and asks, "Y'all finished?"

Hobbs replies, "Yep."

Bentley continues, "You done with it, Hicks?"

"Yes, sir."

Hobbs nods toward Bentley and then looks down to the man on the ground. He extends his hand to help the fellow ranger and grins. "Hicks, you kick like a mule."

Ranger Hicks spits a stream of blood, sucks on his fat lip and reaches his hand up to take the other ranger's offering. "Hobbs... You punch like a donkey." The two dust themselves off and join the rest of the rangers.

Looking at his men, Bentley snorts, "Now that the fun is over, let's move out." He looks to Hobbs and then at Kent. "I want Kent to go along with Hicks to get those kids to town and deliver the captive."

Kent breathes a sigh of relief and nods agreeably. Ranger Hobbs spits aside and puts up his dukes toward the other ranger. "Hey, Kent... You don't want to fight about it?" The comment makes the other rangers chuckle, releasing the built-up tension.

Ranger Bentley lets the laughter settle and continues with, "The rest of us will follow after the marauders and do what we can to put a stop to them." When Jules turns to leave with the others, the captain calls after him, "Mister Ward... Hold it a minute."

With a hard, determined look, the young man turns back to Bentley. The tall ranger captain recognizes the familiar expression and utters, "I suppose you will want to be coming along with us?"

"Yes, sir."

The ranger nods and adds. "T'was a good shot you took that saved Kent yesterday."

"I was just in the right place at the time."

"There are not many folks who will keep their head and stand to fight with a wild, screaming Indian charging straight at them."

"I got nowhere else to be."

Bentley smiles at the matter-of-fact comment and offers a salute. "Nice job, Mister Ward."

"Will that be all? I have horses to tend."

"Yep... That will be all."

The ranger watches Jules return to the job of readying the stock, and looks to his side as Ranger Hobbs approaches. "That is one tough kid..."

"Yeah. I ain't seen one tougher."

"Too bad..."

Hobbs dips his chin in accordance. "Yeah... Growing up all of a sudden will do that to someone." The two rangers resume their tasks, and then mount up to continue on with their duty.

Chapter 15

In Texas hill country, the group of rangers rides north toward the Llano uplift. Jules follows behind the other riders, as they cross Sandy Creek and proceed north to a large dome of granite rock. Tugging the pack mule along behind his horse, he surveils the surroundings while fighting the uncomfortable sensation of being watched.

In the lead, Ranger Hobbs halts his horse, steps down from the saddle and inspects the tracks of the marauders. Looking up to Bentley who is still mounted, he nods to him. "Yep, they come through here all right..." He glances over his shoulder and then back to his captain. "Thought we might've lost their trail when a few split off by the creek, but it picks up again." Letting his gaze search the far distance, Bentley asks, "How many in their group, ya reckon?"

"Appears to be 'bout a dozen or more mounted, and half as many on foot." Hobbs toes the sandy ground. "Judgin' from the shuffle of these tracks, most are prob'ly captives." Ranger Hobbs lifts a boot to his stirrup and climbs back into the saddle. He nudges the flank of his mount and moves over beside Bentley, as they ride on.

Eric H. Heisner

At the back of the group, Jules strains forward to hear what the rangers discuss, but can't make out much of the conversation. He eases alongside one of the younger riders, Corky McCandles, and whispers, "What are they saying?"

"Hell, I cain't hear 'em." Ranger McCandles puts a finger in his ear and gives it a spirited wiggle. "They's prob'ly tryin' to figure out how we can surround them Injuns with only the six of us." Snuffling, the ranger looks over at Jules. "I'd say only five and a half if I hadn't seen you knock down that Comanche with yer pistol shot the other day."

Jules rides along and seems indifferent to the incident. "Just done what anyone would of..." They continue riding behind the others and Corky laughs. "The hell, you say... Kent near shit his britches and has probably had his fill of rangerin' after that jaunt."

The pack mule trails behind, and Jules gives it a tug to motivate it. He looks to Corky, who is about ten years older than himself. "How long you been rangering?"

Corky chews on his tongue and scratches the front of his vest. "I don't know... On and off the past couple years."

"Don't you like being a ranger?"

Corky sniffs and rubs a finger along his nostril. "Sure... I do, but when the state runs out of money, the first thing they do is cut our pay." He smiles at Jules. "I like it well enough, but not so much as to do it for free."

"You have a home to go back to?"

"Yeppers. A real pretty wife and two fine kids."

The two riders travel quietly for a moment, until Jules breaks the lull in conversation. "How come you keep leaving them to do this sort of work?"

Corky leans over in the saddle to Jules and talks low, as if he has a well-kept secret. "I cain't say for other men's wives, but the prettier they are, the harder they are to deal with on a regular basis."

Jules looks confused. "Don't they just do what needs doing and tend to the young'uns?"

The young ranger breaks out laughing, nearly falls from his horse and then replies, "You sure ain't too familiar with womenfolk or havin' a wife."

Hurt shows in the young man's expression, as he reflects on his history with females. Jules answers meekly. "My mother and sisters weren't around for long."

At the head of the procession, Ranger Bentley looks back to sternly shush the two jabbering riders. "You two... Keep quiet back there."

Corky hunkers his head down and grins over at Jules. "Wives are like strong liquor."

"How's that?"

"They'll give ya some pleasure, often followed by a terrible headache, and you only miss 'em when they're gone."

Pondering on this nugget of frontier wisdom for a moment, Jules responds, "I don't drink."

"Cause you don't have a wife..."

The boy looks ahead to the other Texas Rangers. "Hobbs there drinks plenty, and he ain't married."

"Heck, he's been married on and off more than most. Jest not currently, is all..."

The picture of a solitary life as a Texas Ranger begins to come together for Jules, and it doesn't seem all that terrible. The thought of riding after renegades and outlaws without having to deal with the matters of a home appeals to him. Jules looks over at Corky and then to the men riding ahead. "What about Captain Bentley?"

"I don't know much 'bout him on a day to day basis. He don't really share, and no one has the gumption to ask him 'bout his doin's outside of ranger work."

"Maybe he has a wife and ten kids?"

"Doubt it. He ain't the type."

"What is the type?"

Corky glances over at Jules and shrugs nonchalantly. "Folks change over time, of course, but take you for example. The way you are with a six-shooter, mostly keepin' to yerself, I'd say you maybe wouldn't mix well with a regular woman."

The youth glances down to the gun perched on his hip. "What's a gun got to do with it?"

"Most womenfolk like a strong man around the home, but they don't want him too much in control."

"I don't see your meaning?"

Corky grimaces and tries to explain further. "Ya see... I'll kill a man if'n I have to, but the thought troubles me some, and I ain't quick in gettin' there."

Jules stares ahead as they ride, following the others. "No good woman would want me because of what I done?"

Falling back from the group a ways, they try to keep their voices lowered. Corky shakes his head. "Ain't saying that... It's just that I hear you been through some tough times, and it got real bloody."

"You could say that..."

"Like I said, folks can change."

Suddenly, an arrow flies out from the bushes and sticks under the arm of the rider in front of them. The ranger slumps forward in his saddle, and the rider next to him grabs at the horse's bridle to pull it close. An alarm call alerts the ranks. "Injuns!!!"

Chapter 16

Spinning his horse around, Ranger Hobbs draws his sidearm, cocks it and then fires into the brush where the arrow looked to have come from. While his horse nervously skitters aside, he holds the reins tighter and hollers as he waves ahead. "Move on up here, boys, and stick together!" From close by, another arrow whizzes out, and Ranger Hobbs blasts his revolver into the dense brush again.

The horses snort and whinny, as they hustle forward through a cloud of churned-up dust. In the flurry of action, Ranger Bentley draws his rifle from the saddle scabbard, levers a round, and shouts, "Mister Ward! Bring up that mule, or they'll have ya for sure!"

A series of arrows sling through the air past Jules, and two of them stick hard in the packsaddle of food stores. Keeping a grip on the mule's lead rope, Jules kicks his heels hard against his horse's flank and urges the animals forward. In short time, he is clustered behind the arrow-struck ranger and the rider that is pulling him along. Ranger Bentley waves them all past him and points to a mound of rocks to the north. "They're all around us now! Head fast for that high ground with our supplies, and we'll defend our back trail for the wounded."

Spurring his horse onward, Jules charges past the wounded ranger and makes his way up the inclining terrain. The sounds of gunshots echo off the surrounding hills, while arrows whiz past him. Jules scampers his horse and the trailing mule up the slab of rock, and he finds a hollow area where a circle of boulders would make for good defense.

At the entry to the rocky bulwark, Jules leaps from his mount and tethers the lead rope of the mule to a nearby tree. He ground-ties his horse and reaches up to his saddle horn to unhook the cloth sack containing his pistol ammunition. Drawing his pistol, Jules rushes to a defensive position, just as the Texas Ranger leading the wounded man comes up over the ridge and steers toward the tree and the supply mule.

Only steps behind, Corky scampers his horse up the embankment, jumps from his saddle and lands next to Jules. Flushed, and breathing heavily, the ranger notices the youth has his pistol out and aimed down the rocky escarpment. "Where's that Indian-sniffing dog of yourn when we need it?"

Suddenly, Jules realizes that he hasn't seen Dog all day. He shrugs it off as another solitary element of ranger life. "He's what they call, independent."

Ranger McCandles grabs a rifle off his mount, and levers it as he hunkers down beside Jules. He looks back at the other two rangers. One of them secures the horses while the other remains slumped in the saddle. Corky hollers to them. "Get him dismounted, so we can tend to his wound."

With a loaded cartridge belt under his arm and holding a single-shot Sharps, the ranger dashes from the tied horses. He shakes his head grimly. "There is no need to git him down or tend to the wound... He's dead."

Corky looks back at the man with the arrow stuck in the side and bows his head. "Damn... That is some bad luck and sure lessens our odds."

Above the Llano

Jules peeks around the concealing boulders to look down the trail. He whispers quietly to the pair of rangers. "Was Hobbs or Bentley behind you?"

Both rangers shake their heads and, from their vantage, Corky scans the terrain. "Neither of them followed after us." He adds, "Hobbs rode into the brush with pistols a'poppin'." As the three stare across the landscape of scrubby bushes and trees, metal horseshoes scrape the rock as a rider approaches.

From a stand of trees, Ranger Bentley charges toward their position. Like an orchestra conductor's wand, an arrow shaft stuck in his left arm wags up and down as he lopes his horse toward the top of the rocky mound. Jules brightens at the sight of the captain. "Here comes Bentley now…!"

As Ranger Bentley nears, two horseback Comanche warriors in close pursuit suddenly burst from the bushes. Rising from his concealed position, Jules balances his pistol barrel on top of one of the bigger rocks and takes careful aim. He glances over to see that Corky has his rifle cocked and ready at his shoulder. Jules calls out to the ranger, "McCandles, I got the one on the right…"

Almost simultaneously, gunshots from both pistol and rifle explode from the rocks, and the two Indians trailing behind Bentley tumble from their mounts. Levering his rifle, Corky smiles over at Jules. "I'll be damned!"

"Nice shot."

Corky laughs and jests, "Looks like I got 'em both."

"The hell you say!" Jules shakes his head, as Bentley, with the arrow still dangling from his arm, charges past them and hops from his horse. After securing his mount next to the others, Bentley inspects the dead Texas Ranger still horseback. Making his way over to the other ranger, he has a few quiet words with him before looking toward Jules and Corky.

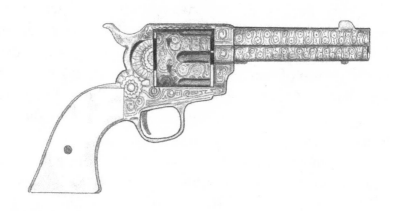

Chapter 17

Keeping low behind the cover of rocks, Ranger Bentley moves in between Corky and Jules. After looking back down the trail, he takes a deep breath, wincing as he glances to the arrow still stuck in his arm. Holding his rifle under the other elbow, he and looks at Corky, who warily queries, "Captain… You okay?"

"Hell no, I ain't okay, McCandles."

Corky averts his gaze from the dangling arrow and asks, "Where's Hobbs?"

"That durned, double-fisted fool is somewhere down there and probably dead by now."

Jules sees the feathered shaft flop and hang limp through Bentley's blood-soaked shirt sleeve. He offers meekly, "Looks like that arrow is only in the fleshy part of yer arm. Want me to cut it out?"

The captain looks down at his bleeding arm before gazing out to the quiet terrain. His attention comes to rest on the dead Comanche and the loose ponies wandering nearby. He turns to address Jules and Corky. "Thanks to you both for the cover fire."

Corky chuckles and gives a sideward gesture to Jules. "I thought I got 'em both, but young Jules there probably got one of 'em with his scratched-up pistol."

Jules grins in reply. "Why don't you go down there and put yer finger in the hole to see whose it was?"

The ranger glances at the captain and then looks down his rifle sights to the covering brush below. He shakes his head and lifts his gaze to look back at Jules. "No thanks, kid. There are probably more than a few hostiles still down there. I'll give you this one."

Ranger Bentley taps Jules on the shoulder and then motions him back toward the tethered horses. "Mister Ward, would you be so kind as to remove this arrow?"

Jules lowers the pistol he has aimed at the brush below. "I think Ranger Hobbs had some medicinal whiskey in the supply packs we can use." The young man flips open the side loading gate of his pistol and ejects the empty shell casing. Reaching into his cloth sack, he pulls out another cartridge and slips it into the empty spot in the cylinder. After snapping the loading gate closed, he rotates the cylinder for the hammer to rest on an empty chamber. Corky watches the boy handle the weapon and comments, "Ya don't load it six-around?"

Jules tilts his head. "Not if I can do the job with five." Holstering the firearm, he creeps over toward the horses. Ranger Bentley follows and moves alongside the pack animal. He grumbles, "Hobbs slipped in a few bottles for emergencies, I suppose..."

Unpacking one of the dark-colored bottles, Jules looks over his shoulder and replies, "Them were his exact words..."

~*~

The day's last rays of sunshine gleam over the hills surrounding the ranch cabin. Inside, Holton sits by the hearth. He places another log on the fire and watches the flames lick up to fight off the darkness. Across the room, Alice works at wetting and reshaping one of Charlie Nichols worn-out hats. Holton glances over at her and nods. "That beaver-felt hat gonna work for ya?"

She pinches the crown, presses it to retain the shape, and looks at him. "It will keep the sun off, for sure."

"It will do that."

Alice puts the hat on, and the oversized fit makes her look like either a comical drunkard or an ugly outlaw-type. She catches her reflection in the pane of window and frowns. "I guess I'm not exactly the appearance of high fashion."

Holton offers an approving grin. "Neither was Charlie. And he don't use it anymore."

A feeble groan comes from the bunk. Rolling over, Bear coughs a spell and then tries to sit up. Placing the hat aside, Alice wipes her hands and moves to the wounded man's bed. "There, there now... You just lay down and rest."

Rising from his chair fireside, Holton peers over at his old friend, adding, "C'mon now... Be still, like she says."

With another moan, Bear lies down again and turns his head to the glow of the fire. "Is that you I hear, Holton?"

"Yeah, Bear... How'r ya doing?"

"Feels like I was gut-shot and turned inside-out."

Grabbing one of the chairs near the table, Holton walks over to sit by Bear's bedside. "Yeah, you caught one good."

As Holton sits down, the incapacitated man turns his head to eye Alice for a moment, and then looks back to his friend. "Thought I was a dead man fer sure, and that one of you was Charlie standin' there."

Holton pats Bear's arm affectionately. "You're a grizzled ol' cuss, but not ready to be dead yet."

Alice moves to pick up Charlie's old hat again and continues to mold it in her hands. Craning his neck to watch,

Bear sighs... "Then, I thought I done saw a glowing angel in my dreams." His faraway gaze turns to Holton, and he frowns dejectedly. "It sure weren't you that I saw."

Exchanging a hopeful look with Alice, Holton nods. "Glad you're feeling some better today." The injured man tries to sit up again but can't muster enough energy. Placing his hand on Bear's shoulder, Holton eases him gently back down to rest again. "Don't go running off on us now..."

"Dammit, I will as soon as I can!"

Holton grins. "Where you got to get in a hurry?"

Wincing from his tender bullet wound, Bear groans. "Finally got yous both set up nice to play house, and now I'm crippled in bed to ruin it for ya."

Holton looks to see Alice discreetly covering a smile with her hand. He directs his attention back to Bear, commenting, "The company in this here cabin will do just fine with you still around."

Bear groans and utters, "Beats diggin' another grave... And, I'll be on my way in a few days."

Holton gives a consenting nod. "Sure ya will, old pal. Now, get some rest so you can heal."

The gruff military scout mumbles a few choice words under his breath and then closes his eyes. Holton rises from the chair and moves back a few steps to stand beside Alice. She glances at him and whispers, "He's better, it seems."

"A little..."

Turning her head so Bear can't overhear, she speaks with a quiet voice. "It will be much more than a couple of days, if his insides are to mend properly."

Concerned, Holton looks down at his old friend recuperating on Charlie's bunk. "We'll just keep him where he's at and hope for the best."

Chapter 18

Hunkered down behind the defensive circle of rocks, the Texas Rangers watch as the afternoon light fades to dusk. Peeking out over a concealing boulder, Jules hears an animal call that is answered in kind. He ducks back, knowing it could be communication between the Indians that surround them. He looks over at Corky, with his rifle cocked and ready, staring out into the darkening countryside. Straining their eyes in the dimming light, they both notice a slight movement in the shadows. Keeping his voice low, Jules hisses at Corky. "You see 'im?"

"Yep." The ranger's rifle hammer drops, and the fiery blast lights up the evening as it roars across the landscape. They hear rustling in the brush, but there is no one to be seen. Aiming his pistol, Jules murmurs, "Did ya get 'im?"

"Dunno..."

His arm in a sling, Ranger Bentley crouches low and scampers over to their position. "Are they making a move?"

Corky looks to the ranger captain and shakes his head. "Nothing yet... Me and the kid here have been watching one sneak forward for the last hour or so."

"Ya hit anything with that shot?"

"Could have..."

When another rustling sound comes from the bushes, Corky levers his rifle again and takes aim. He glances over toward Jules, as the boy levels his pistol barrel on top of the large boulder before him. As all three squint into the darkness, they hear a familiar voice call out to them. "Don't shoot, dammit... It's me!"

Ranger Hobbs suddenly explodes from the brush and runs full tilt up the rocky escarpment to the ranger holdout. An arrow zips past his shoulder and several flashing gunshots light up the terrain around him. A Comanche brave leaps from the bushes, about to tackle Hobbs, when a growling canine sweeps the legs from under the warrior, knocking him to the ground.

Spurs a' jangling, Hobbs makes his way to the top of the rocky dome and briefly looks back, as Dog viciously snarls and bites at the cowering Indian. Just before reaching safety, another warrior dashes from the brush with a raised war club. Before he swings it down on the ranger, simultaneous gunshots from the rocks above stop him dead in his tracks.

Flashing his pearly-white teeth, Corky looks over. "Damn, Jules! It was surely my shot that got 'im that time!"

Jules shakes his head and cocks the hammer of his pistol again. "Sure it was..."

Finding cover amongst the rocks, Ranger Hobbs murmurs, "Thanks, boys..."

Bentley grumbles, "Glad you come to join us."

Smirking, Hobbs adds. "It's not like I run off or somethin'. Ain't no saloons nearby..."

The captain squats next to Hobbs and gives him a sideways glance. "If there was, you'd find it."

Their playful banter is interrupted by snarling yaps and several distant gunshots. Jules stands and calls over the rocks.

"Dog... Dog!" Cupping a hand around his mouth, he hollers, "Up here...! Come on, boy!"

The mongrel dog runs up the steep escarpment toward the rangers' position. Several arrows shoot out from the bushes, and Dog yelps painfully when one of them catches him in the hindquarters. Ranger Bentley aims and fires into the brush, yelling, "Give that dog some cover fire."

Corky, Bentley and Jules let off shot after shot, as Dog clambers up the rocks to safety. Once the shooting has stopped, Ranger Hobbs looks to the others and grunts, "Damn, boys...You give a hell of a lot better cover fire for that four-legged beast than you did for me."

Using just one hand, Bentley reloads his revolver and smiles at Hobbs. "He was running a lot faster, too."

Hobbs snaps back. "Well, he's got more legs!"

With soothing words, Jules carefully approaches Dog and attempts to inspect the canine's injured flank. "Easy there, fella... Glad you made it." The dog cowers and whimpers, as he licks at where the arrow shaft protrudes from his thigh. "Easy there boy... We got to get that sticker pulled out of ya." Jules continues to murmur softly to the dog, as the others split their attention between the surrounding terrain and the wounded animal.

Hobbs slides a cartridge in the loading gate of his rifle. "That's a useful dog, but I sure don't think I'd get near to him when he's wounded."

Bentley gives the ranger a swat and shushes him. "Hobbs, you talk too much."

They all watch as Jules slowly reaches out to the arrow. Dog growls a pained warning, as Jules cautiously touches his fingers to the wooden shaft and explains, "I don't want to hurt you, Dog... We got to get this arrow out though." There's a low, rumbling growl that raises hairs on each ranger's neck, but Jules stands his ground. Holding firmly onto the arrow shaft, he lifts up his other empty hand, open-palmed, toward the dog's muzzle. "Dog… This might hurt something awful, but you'll feel a whole lot better when it's done…" Sharply snapping his fingers as a distraction, he jerks the arrow free.

Chapter 19

Dog snaps his jaws in the air and yelps. He jumps to his feet and circles around looking to find the arrow that is now free from his hindquarter. Jules stands and quickly takes a few steps backward. He holds the arrow out to show the animal. "Easy Dog... It's out now."

The dog's dark eyes twinkle in the fading light, as he stares at the boy and the offending object. With a slight moan, the canine reaches back to lick his wound. Then, he limps off to the shelter of the nearest thicket. Jules takes a deep breath and tosses the arrow aside.

Moving back to the group of rangers, Jules draws his pistol and takes his guard position again. Nearby, Corky leans on the rock face with his rifle and grins over toward Jules. "You still got all yer fingers? Better count 'em to be sure..."

Jules glances down at his hands and then holds the pistol to his chest to calm the tremble. "Someone had to do it."

Hobbs speaks out from across the defensive rocks. "You sure weren't gonna get any volunteers."

Ranger Bentley handles his gun with his good hand, looks to his sling and then gives an affirming nod to Jules. "Nice work, again, Mister Ward. Now, take it easy and rest. We'll see if we can get clear of here in the morning."

Everyone settles in for a brief respite from the fighting. All around them, the night is filled with various animal calls. The sound of a hooting owl or coyotes yipping, seem to be possible communication between the natives and sends chills down their spines. Jules scans the darkness a while and slowly lets his eyes close. He listens into the night before finally drifting off.

~*~

As the sun begins to crest over the horizon, Jules sits on watch, still hunkered down in his position. Pistol held close, the youth looks around at the small group of Texas Rangers. Then, he looks over to the arrow shaft on the ground that was pulled out of the injured dog the night prior.

In the light of a new day, the outnumbered band of rangers are faced with the harsh reality of their predicament. Having had little or no sleep, the defenders are still on alert. At a nearby mound of rocks, Corky snorts himself awake after having briefly drifted off. In a panic, he looks around, gradually calming himself when he realizes that there is no imminent danger. After checking his weapon, he whispers over to Jules. "Hey… You awake?"

"Yeah…You sleep any?"

"Not much."

The boy pulls his coat tighter to fend off the morning chill and asks, "What do you think we'll do?"

The ranger holds his rifle closer to his chest, shivers momentarily and shrugs. "I sure ain't the brains of this outfit. I'll leave the hard thinkin' up to them others."

Across the defensive circle, Ranger Bentley and Hobbs quietly discuss their limited options. They look to young Jules and the other two Texas Rangers, and then to the body lain out on the ground next to the pack mule and saddle horses.

Above the Llano

Jules turns his gaze to the landscape and notices that the dead Comanche from the evening's battle are now absent. He whispers over to Corky. "It looks like they took their dead. Maybe they moved on?"

Corky looks out to where the two bodies had been. "Damn... They nearly climbed up here with us, and we didn't even hear 'em."

They exchange a baffled look, as Bentley, Hobbs and the other ranger make their way over to them. Jules lowers his pistol and shakes his head at Corky. "We won't go another night as lucky."

Keeping his head low, huddling close to the others, Ranger Bentley cradles his injured arm, as he looks to Corky and Jules. "How did you boys do for sleep last night?"

Despite being exhausted from the lack of shut-eye, Jules puts on a positive countenance. "Fine, sir."

Corky nods his agreement, and watches Hobbs come up alongside Bentley. Looking questioningly to the captain, Ranger Hobbs squats to his spurs and asks, with a cheery air, "Hey there, fellas... We gonna skedaddle out of here today?"

Bentley replies, "It seems we have only a few options."

Corky peeks over the rocks, scans the horizon, and then looks back at the group. "The only two that I can see are... stick here and fight, or flee."

All the rangers nod in agreement, until Jules coughs and adds, "We could attack them."

Gazing fondly toward the boy, Ranger Hobbs snickers. "I like the way this boy thinks." He glances over his shoulder to where Dog watches them attentively from the bushes. "...and that mangy mutt of his, too."

Ranger Bentley peers out at the hostile terrain and tilts his head dejectedly. "We don't have the numbers to attack, nor do we know their position enough to successfully retreat."

The captain turns his attention to the dead man by the horses. "Today, we'll need to get him buried the best we can and then keep to this advantaged position. My thought is to have the horses saddled and ready if we get overrun."

The ranger behind Bentley keeps his gaze scanning the landscape and queries, "Do you think they'll lose interest and maybe move on?"

Hobbs responds candidly. "We trailed 'em this far and will do it again, so they have nothin' to gain by leavin' us be."

"I could ride for help." Everyone looks at Jules, admiring his gumption, but Hobbs and Bentley exchange a look and dismiss the notion.

With his uninjured arm, Bentley gestures to the north. "The closest help might be Fort Mason."

Hobbs interjects. "Prob'ly over forty miles..."

"We will be better off holding to our positions here and keeping at the ready."

Disappointed by their reaction, the boy turns away from the rangers and looks out to the surrounding territory. "We'll surely be short of water by the end of the day."

Considering the loaded supply mule, Bentley replies. "We'll be on tight rations until we get clear of here." The captain looks at Jules and then tilts his head toward Hobbs. "Mister Ward, would you mind helping Hobbs with burying the dead and tending to our mounts?"

"Yes, sir."

Bentley looks around at the few under his command. "Keep your eyes and ears sharp. Conserve food and bullets. This is a good spot, and we should be able to defend it well." Nodding in agreement, everyone moves back to their guard positions. Jules follows after Hobbs to help with the horses and to put their dead companion in the ground.

Chapter 20

At the old Nichols homestead, Holton works near the barn. His attention turns to the cabin, as Alice steps out and goes to the water well with a wood bucket. Sensing that he is watching her, she glances over at him and continues her task. They both try to keep to their work, while each occasionally sneaks glances over at the other. After she finishes filling the water bucket, Alice returns to the cabin and goes inside. Holton tosses a hammer into a wooden box, muttering, "Dang-nabbit... Having a woman around this place is more distracting than anything else..."

A chill runs through him, when he hears the cabin door creak open again. He looks up to see Alice step out and stand at the front edge of the porch. The independent-minded woman dries her hands on her apron and stares in his direction for a good length of time. Her mind set, she unties her apron, sets it on the railing and descends the porch stairs. Holton turns away and resumes his work. He pretends not to notice her approaching, all the while, feeling his heart thump and his pulse beat quicker.

The soft tread of her footsteps stop when she is directly behind him. He glances over his shoulder at her and comments, "It takes longer with you watching.

"Why is that?"

Pivoting around to face her, Holton astutely assesses Alice before responding. "That's just the way things go."

Admiring his handy-work, she smiles at Holton. "Mister Lang, do you like being a rancher?"

He shrugs. "I ain't really done much ranching ever. Most'a what's left of Charlie's herd is probably scattered from here to California."

"You've rounded up some of them."

"What few I've brought home from jaunts of hunting ain't much."

The woman standing before him reaches her hands behind her neck and lifts her long hair up off her shoulders. "It's been warming up lately."

He casts his gaze to the position of the sun in the sky. "Summer will be on us soon."

There is an awkward pause in conversation, and Alice glances to the shaded interior of the barn. She looks back to Holton in his sweaty work clothes and thinks back to him sewing on his buckskin shirt. "You lived with the Apache?"

"I did for quite a few of my younger years."

"Did you have a wife?"

An odd sensation suddenly comes over him, as he responds reticently to the personal inquiry. "I did at that." They exchange a look of mutual understanding, and she continues to stare at him in a loving way that would unsettle any man's nerves.

Alice casts her gaze away. "I was married, before... With children..." Holton nods once, and she continues with, "Did you like having a wife?"

Unsure how to answer, he follows her stare to the barn. "There were some benefits."

"Would you like to show me?"

"Possibly..."

Swallowing the rising lump in his throat, Holton looks to the cabin. As if reading his mind, Alice brushes past him, steps into the shade of the barn, and whispers as she passes. "Bear is resting peacefully now and will be for some time."

He watches her go inside and then wait for him near one of the stalls. Without another word, Holton follows after her and gently swings the repaired barn door closed.

~*~

Gunshots fill the breeze with smoke from burnt black-powder charges. From all sides, mounted Comanche braves scramble up and down the rocky embankment leading to the position of the holed-up rangers. Jules cradles his pistol in his lap and reloads from his supply of ammo in the flour sack. Next to him, Corky levers his rifle again and takes careful aim. The ranger mutters under his breath. "Damn all those red-skinned bastards..."

Jules slips a cartridge into the sixth chamber of his handgun and snaps the loading gate closed. "Heck, it ain't their fault we're here on their land."

Corky gives Jules a sideways glance and grumbles. "Sure ain't our fault that they murdered them farmin' folks..." Jules shifts his position to peer out over the rocks toward the attackers below. "Don't waste yer lead if you can help it." Corky nods and quickly ducks back, as an arrow skitters off a rock near his face. "They sure ain't holding back..."

As the two exchange an anxious look, Jules mutters, "Maybe they are..."

Chapter 21

The arrows continue to probe the area for targets, while bullet lead tears through the brush. Jules looks around at the small group of Texas Rangers hunkered down behind rocks. He pokes his head up to look at the attackers and raises the barrel of his gun to take aim.

The Comanche warriors dart in and out of the bushes, gradually closing in. Jules patiently watches and holds his fire, selecting a target. An arrow arcs through the sky and clatters down between Jules and Corky. The ranger's eyes widen, and he slips several more cartridges into the magazine of his rifle. He counts the remaining ammunition on his cartridge belt and notices Jules still waiting for a clear shot. "Are you going to let 'em get close enough to throw rocks or do something with that fancy shooter?!?"

Jules stays focused as he waits on taking the shot. Finished reloading, Corky levers the rifle and takes aim at a Comanche charging up toward them. Just before the ranger squeezes the trigger, Jules makes the shot and the mounted Indian tumbles off his horse to lie still on the ground.

The youth offers a playful wink to the surprised ranger. "I suppose you got that one, too, without even squeezin' the trigger."

Corky levers his long gun, and a bullet-tipped cartridge ejects out the top to land on the ground between them. Looking at Jules, he smiles sheepishly. "I'll be gol-danged if you ain't a pretty good shot with that scratched-up shooter…"

Jules grabs the cartridge from the ground and tosses it to Corky, who catches it against his vest and then slides it back into the side loading gate of his rifle. The two resume taking alternating shots at the attacking Indians until, finally, all falls quiet.

The thick cloud of black-powder smoke hanging in the air slowly dissipates. Corky looks back and sees that one of the horses is down with an arrow through the throat. "Damn… They got one of the horses."

Jules turns toward the mounts and notices multiple arrows stuck upright in the ground. He surmises that keeping the horses saddled had prevented even more arrow injuries. He stares at a feathered shaft stuck in a leather saddle skirt and comments, "Once they can keep us from being horseback, all they have to do is wait us out…"

"Them murderin' red-devils sure know how to make a person feel unwelcome."

Jules smiles, as he slips a few more cartridges into his pistol cylinder to replace the spent ones. "You'd do the same in your own home."

"My home ain't so big."

As the smoke from the gunfight lingers and then wafts away, Jules scans the vast horizon. He slides down behind the rock and mutters, "Their's ain't so much either, anymore…"

~*~

The fighting has stopped, and the quiet gives way to the chatter of birds and insects. Ranger Bentley leads the other rangers nearer to Corky and Jules, where the main attack was focused. Surveilling the terrain, he squats down next to them. "How are you boys holding up?"

Ranger McCandles smiles and gestures toward Jules. "Cap, we should give the kid a rifle 'n see what he can do."

Hobbs looks over Bentley's shoulder down to the dead Comanche on the rocks and another in the brush further on. Impressed, he nods to Jules. "You get them with yer pistol?"

Before Jules can answer, Corky pats his Winchester and grins. "Unless I got me a magic rifle that saves on bullets." When they look to him in confusion, he explains. "Jules is the one who done 'em in. Cool as a cucumber."

Ranger Hobbs puts his hand to the boy's shoulder and smiles over at Bentley. "See, Bent? I knew it was a good idea to bring this kid along."

The captain grimaces and looks over to the dead horse. "It appears they have us surrounded and are determined to get our horses one way or another."

Hobbs squats near to his spurs and gives one of the rowels a spin. "And they'll do it, too, if we stick around here much longer." One of the rangers holds up his wooden canteen and gives the remaining water a hollow swish. "Yeah, we're near out of our supply of water too."

The group falls quiet, as Ranger Bentley ponders their situation. Finally, he looks up to each man and speaks in a low voice that will not carry far. "We'll move out tonight, just after full dark, and take our chances to the north."

Ranger Hobbs adds, "Most likely they'll hit us again before that, so take every measure to protect them animals. Unless you're keen on goin' afoot…"

Bentley looks to Jules and Corky. "As it stands now, we're a bit shy on our riding stock. One of you will have to fork that supply mule. Strip that saddle and tack off the dead animal, and see if that critter will take to bridle."

87

Jules nods dutifully, but Ranger McCandles gives an unhappy look toward Hobbs and grumbles, "Maybe the feller who come runnin' up here without his horse should throw a leg over the jackass…"

The more experienced ranger glares at Corky and spits. "McCandles, do I have to stomp you and put you in yer place like I done Hicks?"

Somebody snickers. Hobbs looks around to see Jules holding back a giggle. "What are you laughing at, kid?"

"Just not sure who got the trouncing on that affair…"

"You want next in line?"

Composing himself, Jules utters, "I'll save ya the trouble and ride the mule."

Hobbs stares at Jules for a moment and can't help but smile at the boy's youthful willingness. "Kid, you sure are a game son-of-a… I don't know what!"

From the bushes, Dog's grumbling bark seems to agree with the ranger, but serves to alert them to somebody moving in the brush below. Jules gets low behind the boulders and peers out. "They're coming at us again."

Bentley waves Hobbs and the other rangers back to their positions and whispers loudly to them all. "Remember! Do your best to protect them mounts." Raising his good arm, he cocks back the hammer on his pistol and fires a shot into the rocky scrub below. As if a switch has been triggered, the Comanche commence another round of attacks.

Chapter 22

Seated in the rocking chair on the porch of the cabin, Bear looks out at the colorful evening sky. He hears the pop of a gunshot in the distance and perks his ears in that direction. After a while, Alice comes out of the cabin and puts her hands into the pockets in the front of her apron. He notices that she stares longingly out to the faraway hills.

Before long, over the hilltop, a horseback figure appears silhouetted against the brilliant sunset. Holton rides down toward the cabin with a pair of jackrabbits tied together by their hind legs and draped over the withers of his horse. Bear watches his friend approach, and then looks to Alice as she admires the rider's every move.

Easing his horse up to the front porch, Holton halts his mount and hands the two long-legged critters over to Alice. She looks at them tenderly and smiles to Holton in a familiar way before taking the meat inside to prepare for dinner. Bear watches the obvious display of affection most curiously. Sitting silently, he waits as Holton climbs down from his horse to take a seat on the porch steps. Rocking back and forth in his chair, Bear peers inside to Alice skinning the rabbits and then looks to Holton on the stairs. "How long exactly have I been dead to the world?"

Holton looks up at Bear, thinks on it and then remarks, "Jest a few days more'n a week or so."

Bear scratches his beard and tugs at his chin whiskers. "You know, Holton. I ain't never seen someone look so appreciative for a pair of stringy jackrabbits."

Pivoting on the stair tread, Holton perceptibly blushes. He glances to his old friend and then looks away to the sky. "Rabbit stew must be one of her favorites."

Rubbing the stem of his clay pipe between his fingers, Bear grunts, "Yeah... That, or somethin' else..." Holton stands up and steps onto the porch to take a seat in the ladder-back chair next to Bear. The recently wounded scout puts his empty pipe between his teeth and sucks air. He narrows a questioning eye at Holton. "I kin tell somethin' is different."

"Yeah?"

"Ya know she's been laying lovin' eyes on you since the day ya first met."

"Hmm?"

Bear tilts his head back, looks down his nose at Holton, and whispers, "How long has it been since you started lovin' back on her?"

Holton smiles bashfully and looks at Alice through the cabin window. "Just happened recent..."

The old cavalry scout takes the pipe from between his teeth and taps it on his leg. "I knowed it right off!"

"Hush now or she'll hear you talk."

Bear smirks and rocks his chair forward to take another look inside at Alice. A troubled expression suddenly crosses his features as he rocks back, whispering aside to his friend. "You ain't been at it while I was in there laid up, was you?"

Holton thinks a moment, shakes his head and mutters, "I ain't done it in a house since I was... Come to think on it, I don't think I've ever done it inside a proper house."

"Well, damnation! I'm gonna sleep in the barn 'n leave y'all to it." Holton smiles, as he gazes over to the barn door. Bear picks up on his blissful rumination and shakes his head. "Damn, Holton! You sure know how to romance a gal..."

With a tilt of his head, Holton turns to look at Bear. "Sure wouldn't mind talkin' about somethin' else."

The old scout pats his wounded side, wincing at the tender spot. "Not sure where I'd go yet, but I don't wanna stick 'round here with you's both makin' a love nest."

"Womenfolk can git lonely too, I guess." Holton keeps his voice low. "No need for you to be rushin' off, if she has a mind to leave as well."

"She say she was goin' somewhere?"

"Not directly..."

"Well, it's hard to figure sometimes what a woman says and what they mean."

Holton nods and glances at Alice through the window. "Yeah, and she ain't said much..."

~*~

Darkness has fallen around the defensive circle of rocks, and the small group of Texas Rangers are mounted up, ready to depart. In an effort to make a silent exit, torn cloth has been wrapped around the horses' hooves to dull the sound of metal shoes on the rocky terrain. They quietly ride into the night, leaving behind the shallow grave of their companion and the dead carcass of a horse.

At the rear of the string of riders, astride the long-eared mule, Jules whistles low and quietly calls. "Dog... Dog..." Ranger McCandles tosses him a warning gaze, and they ride on in silence.

Chapter 23

A small spark flashes in the dark. The cloth foot covering on one of the ranger horses has worn through, and the metal shoe strikes against small pieces of flint on the rock-strewn terrain. Using the stars and moon to guide them, the group of rangers quietly marches onward.

Following the single-file line of riders, Jules keeps one hand on the holstered pistol at his side, while he strains his eyes to see in the darkness. Only the soft jangle of brass cartridges in the sack hung from his pommel and the creaking of saddle tack challenge the silence. He turns in the saddle, when he hears a soft rustling in the bushes. The scruffy dog emerges from the underbrush to follow the group. With a twinkle in his eyes, Dog stares up to the boy. Jules can't help but smile, as he looks fondly down at the independent canine.

Ahead, Ranger Bentley and Ranger Hobbs halt the group, and Jules prods the mule on to join them. There is an unspoken tension, as each man peers into the quiet night. Hobbs looks down at Dog and nods approvingly to Jules. "That ugly dog sticking close is a good sign at least."

One of the men clears his throat and lowly whispers, "Why are we stopping?"

With moonlight casting a glow over his features, Ranger Bentley looks toward the northeast. "There is a small creek crossing ahead, and it is a likely place for an ambush."

Corky looks nervously over his shoulder and then back toward the captain. "Why don't we just avoid it altogether and head back to Austin?"

Bringing his horse around to face the group, Ranger Hobbs pushes back his hat. "Because it's not our job to turn tail and skedaddle home." Bentley nods silently and lets Hobbs finish. "Most likely this band of marauders is sticking close to our trail and will remain so." In spite of the darkness, the men can feel his eyes upon them. "The sooner we get to reinforcements the better."

Jules peers down at the dog and notices him still favoring his wounded hindquarter. Dog stares up at him while panting quietly. Jules looks to the group and comments, "Maybe we should split up and cross at two different spots?"

With interest, the rangers all turn to the boy, and Corky speaks out. "Jules, decreasing our numbers and increasing their odds against us don't seem the right thing to do exactly."

When the rangers look to their leader, Bentley asks. "What exactly did you have in mind, Mister Ward?"

Nudging the mule forward, Jules keeps his voice low. "If they're watching us, they already know our numbers are few and can pick a spot to their advantage for an attack." Conveying confidence beyond his age, Jules continues to address them. "Having us split up adds a level of uncertainty for them."

Ranger Hobbs tilts his head and glances to Bentley. "The kid is right. We don't have much to turn the advantage except to confuse 'em."

The rangers sit in silence until Bentley finally speaks. "Hobbs, take McCandles and Ward with you. We'll split ways

94

before crossing and meet on the other side." His saddle creaks as he adjusts his positioning. "Any sound of an engagement, we'll circle around and come at them on the flank."

There is a sense of hesitation, as they nod their understanding. Moving out in single file again, they proceed onward into the darkness.

~*~

Just before reaching the floodplain, Ranger Bentley and the other Texas Ranger split off from the group and move away to the west. The cover of night quickly consumes the two riders and only the footfalls of their horses on the sandy ground can be heard. Soon, all is quiet again.

Ranger Hobbs, with Corky following, rides in the lead, while Jules comes up behind. Dog, limping from his wound, suddenly stops, lifts an ear, and listens. Detecting Dog's halt, Jules looks back. He holds up his mule when he hears a warning growl. "Hear that fellas...?" Corky stops his mount and quietly calls, "Hold it Hobbs, something is up..."

Ranger Hobbs holds his horse and turns to the others. He waits, as Corky and Jules catch up. "What is it, fellas?"

Gesturing toward the alerted mutt, Jules whispers, "Dog is warning us of Indians."

Ranger Hobbs looks at the grumbling dog and nods. "Yeah, we already know there are damned Indians around."

Looking back at Dog sniffing the air, Jules bites his lip and puts his hand to the handle of his gun. "They're close."

His eyes straining into the darkness, Corky comments, "Yeah, he seems to know when they're gonna give us trouble. That is one handy dog for sniffin' Injuns."

Slipping his sidearm from its holster, Hobbs nods his consent. "We can't jest let Bentley cross and then leave 'em high 'n dry. We'll just have to keep on and be ready."

When Corky draws his pistol too, Jules follows his example. The ranger looks to Jules and then over to Hobbs. Wondering aloud, Corky asks them, "How do we go at it? Quick or slow?"

Despite the dim light, they can both see a smile cross Hobbs' features as he responds. "Well, boys... Whichever is the way you want to face death."

Corky murmurs, "Whenever I get into it with the wife, it's usually better to just go at it direct and get it over with, or she'll punish ya for months."

Hobbs clicks back the hammer of his pistol and holds it at the ready. "Quick it is, then..."

McCandles glances at Jules and then looks ahead. "Thing is, I'd much rather have a go at them Indians anytime than have another row with the woman at home."

They each choke up on the length of their reins, hunker down in their saddles and ready themselves to charge. Nodding to the riders beside him, Ranger Hobbs points his pistol forward and clenches his heels hard into his horse's flanks. He lets out a whooping holler, as he lunges ahead. "Heeyaa!!! Let's go...!"

Chapter 24

The riders charge ahead toward the water crossing. Launching over the embankment, they drop into the stream and splash through the shallow waters to the other side. Before they can climb out of the sandy wash, the whiz of an arrow cuts through the night and a cracking gunshot follows. Muzzle blasts light up the dark sky, and the popping report of firearms erupt from both sides of the creek bed. Corky's horse tumbles down and tosses the ranger into the slow-moving current. Jules steers his galloping mule toward the dismounted ranger while firing his pistol in the direction of the gunfire from the shore.

Before Jules reaches Corky, the ranger splashes through the stream to come up alongside Ranger Hobbs, who is firing his pistol slow and deliberate at selected targets. Hobbs kicks his foot out of the stirrup and reaches down to help Corky up. "Mount up, McCandles! Let's git the hell out of here...!" Corky uses the empty stirrup to climb up behind Hobbs, and the horse leaps the last splashing strides to the river bank. Laden with two riders, the horse struggles but finally manages to make it up the embankment, goaded by slaps from the ranger behind the cantle.

Jules turns the mule to follow. He does his best to see beyond the bright bursts of gunfire that mar his vision.

Several more rounds of gunshots erupt from downstream, and Jules can faintly make out the mounted figures of the two other Texas Rangers racing to their aid. Jules aims, fires his pistol and then cocks it again. When he pulls the trigger this time, he hears the hammer click down on an empty chamber. As he kicks the mule's flanks to charge it up the riverbank, he hears the sound of more horses coming, close behind. Ahead, Corky looks back, waves and hollers, "C'mon Jules...

As Jules scampers up the embankment, he sees a muzzle flash to his right, and the mule beneath him instantly drops to its knees and tumbles. The boy is thrown forward, but holds tight to his pistol. Dashing back to the wounded animal struggling on the bank of the stream, Jules jerks his sack of cartridges from the saddle horn.

Momentarily blinded by the flashes of gunfire, Jules doesn't notice when a Comanche steps from behind a tree to take aim at him with a carbine. Running toward the Indian, Jules sees him too late. With a growling snap of canine jaws, Dog tackles the warrior just before the rifle shot goes off. Blinking away the bright spots obscuring his night vision, Jules mutters, "Thanks again, Dog..." His pistol and sack of cartridges clutched close, he ducks down and clambers into the concealing brush. Heaving for breath, he listens as the skirmish wanes. As the occasional pop of gunfire comes from behind him, he scurries away from the creek-side encounter.

~*~

Seated at the rough-plank table, Holton sits opposite Bear while Alice serves them breakfast. Bear packs his pipe and is about to light it, when Alice deliberately removes it from his mouth and places it on top of the fireplace mantle.

Slack-jawed, he follows her with his eyes. "Uhh... Excuse me, ma'am?"

Above the Llano

Alice serves her plate of food last and takes a seat between the two men. "We'll not have smoking at the table while we eat."

Bear gives Holton a look and grimaces. "Since when?"

"Since now…"

The crusty old military scout is obviously taken aback, but begins to eat despite the meddling decree. Holton takes a deep breath, looks to the two at the table and finally speaks. "Is there any other restrictions we need to be made aware of?"

Alice finishes chewing, looks at Holton and smiles. "That's all for now."

With a stern expression, Holton replies, "I'm a mind that it should be all… for good."

She puts down her spoon, looks to Bear, and then to Holton. "I think it is fair for whoever serves the meal to make a small, simple request."

Holton glances to Bear's pipe perched on the mantle. "Is that what it was?"

She looks at him strangely. "Is what, what it was?"

"A request?"

Starting to get her dander up, Alice turns to Bear who slinks down in his chair as he continues to eat his breakfast. She casts a glare toward Holton. "You are both welcome to take your breakfast outside, and smoke as you please."

Holton remains firm. "I'll eat where I please and do as I see fit." He returns her stare. "I don't put demands on others and expect the same courtesy from them." Across the table, Bear, uncomfortable with being in the presence of the marital-like spat, chews a mouthful of food and squirms in his seat. He coughs and splutters. "I'll smoke outside during mealtime. No offense meant by my dirty ol' bachelor habits."

His blood rising, Holton looks at Bear and then at Alice. "When a person goes to makin' demands, they begin small.

99

The next thing you know, they have a list of 'em as long as your arm and are hardly tolerable to be around anymore."

Alice lifts her utensil and begins to eat her meal again. "I don't enjoy smoking while I eat. Never have."

Holton stands and goes over to take Bear's pipe down from the fireplace mantle. "That is fine, and I can understand. I don't like it much myself." He sets the pipe on the table before Bear and sits down again.

Alice looks at the pipe and back to Holton. "And what is that supposed to mean?"

Holton replies coolly. "You're welcome to take your breakfast outside if you like."

Clenching her jaw, Alice glances at Bear, who avoids eye contact. Then, she lifts her plate and walks to the door. She hesitates at the threshold, silently fuming, before moving outside to continue with her breakfast.

Holton looks across the table at Bear and cracks a grin. "You may smoke if you'd like."

Bear stirs the remainder of food on his plate and utters, "I kinda lost my taste for it at the moment." With a nod, Holton continues eating. Bear stares at the food on his plate, then looks across the table at Holton and crinkles his brow. "Ya know, ya prob'ly jest cut off that trail of honey you'd been enjoyin' of late…"

Holton finishes chewing a mouthful and gazes outside. "I don't put unjust demands on others, and I expect them not to be put upon me."

"I can sure say you sound like a longtime bachelor."

"Maybe so…" Holton takes another bite, chews a while, swallows and then remarks, "I never found it necessary for someone to inflict their ways on others."

Bear finishes with his meal and pushes the plate aside. He takes up his pipe, clenches it in his teeth and stares ahead.

Above the Llano

Sliding a matchstick from his pocket, he is about to strike it, then, he thinks better of it and stands up from his chair. Taking the pipe from his teeth, he glances out the door to where Alice eats on the stoop. "I think I'll go smoke behind the barn where I won't bother anyone."

Holton looks up from his plate of breakfast and nods. "You're welcome to do as you please."

Chapter 25

The next day, Jules walks through the brushy terrain with his pistol in hand and the sack of cartridges tucked in his belt. Coming up behind, Dog trots along with a gimp in his gait. Suddenly, a deer flushes from the thicket and startles Jules, freezing him in his tracks.

The boy looks down at the canine and heaves a sigh. "Dog, I sure hope them others are better off than we are." Having a seat, the dog reaches back to lick at his leg wound. Jules studies the hill-covered landscape and listens carefully for any sign of the Texas Rangers. Finally, Jules looks at Dog, tilts his head forward and walks on.

Night falls, and Jules continues to trudge onward. While pushing his way through some bee-brush, he notices the glow of firelight reflected on a rocky bluff in the distance. In disbelief, he stops, looks back at Dog and whispers, "Someone has a cook-fire going."

Dog lets out a rumbling growl and then limps ahead. Jules shrugs and offers, "It wouldn't hurt to find out who." They quietly continue to make their way through the dark, slowly approaching the distant campfire.

Jules creeps through the brush, getting as close as possible without detection, to peer into the camp below the rock bluff. He spots a small group of hostages, with their hands tightly bound, seated by a pond of spring-fed water. Scanning the band of Comanche warriors mingling fireside, he estimates there to be over a dozen.

His jaw clenched, Jules cocks his pistol hammer back. He looks at Dog, and the canine lets out a low, muffled growl. The boy gives a reprimanding look and whispers, "Quiet Dog, I see 'em..."

When Jules turns back to observe the hostages in the camp, he surprisingly comes face to face with a Comanche. Attracted by movement in the brush, the native sentry appears as shocked as the boy. They stare at one another for a split second before the warrior calls out. Jules fires his pistol, silencing the warrior with a single shot.

The gunshot attracts everyone's attention, and the camp quickly scatters. Jules' first instinct is to rush toward the pony herd, but the presence of several braves turns him away. With his pistol in one hand, Jules draws his knife with the other and makes his way toward the hostages instead. Dashing into the camp, the firelight flickers on his features as he slices the bindings and urges the captives to run. "Go now, and git out of here! There are several Texas Rangers about..." The air fills with the chilling cries of mounted warriors tearing through the brush.

Several of the freed captives scurry into the darkness, while Dog attacks a guarding hostile with snaps and growls. Suddenly, a warrior grabs Jules by the shirt collar and arm. When he violently swings him around, Jules slices out with his blade before tumbling away. Grappling desperately with his larger opponent, Jules loses grip on his knife and pistol. Knocked to the ground again, and trying to catch his breath, the boy sees his gun lying under a bush and crawls toward it. The Indian grabs Jules' foot and drags him. Kicking violently with his other leg he breaks the Indian's grip.

Jules sees the Comanche pull back, and then hears something coming from the bushes directly behind him. Turning, he calls out, "Help me... Dog! Are you there...?!?" When a searing pain slams across his young shoulders, Jules looks up to see another Comanche holding a heavy stick, readied to strike it down again. Jules scoots away, clamoring to regain his feet, as the tree branch swings hard against him. The blow to the side of his head tumbles Jules to the ground with pain and blurred vision, before he finally blacks-out to unconsciousness.

Chapter 26

Holton walks up to the cabin and is greeted with a peculiar look from Bear. The old scout leaning on the porch post turns to look behind at Alice, her bags all packed, stepping out from the cabin doorway. She has a troubled look on her face. Holton stops at the bottom stair of the porch, looks up at them and comments, "What's going on? Y'all leaving?"

Comically, and almost simultaneously, they both reply: "I am, and she's staying." "He's staying, I'm going."

Confused by the mixed message, Holton tilts his head and makes his way up the steps. "Just hold on a minute and tell me what happened." The two back away from the stairs, making room for Holton to pass by and take a seat.

Looking to Bear, Alice is the first to explain. "I'm not needed here anymore."

Holton rocks back in the chair, glances to Bear and then looks back to Alice. "How do you figure?"

"Bear is up and about now, and you don't want anyone interfering with your independent lifestyle."

"Those are both true, but it don't mean you have to leave here because of it."

Bear grunts his agreement and takes up a chair by the rocker. As he looks back and forth between Holton and Alice, he grumbles, "There is no need for me to be here to cause problems between yous both." When Holton gives him a look of mocking disbelief, Bear responds with, "What…?!?"

"Bear, where else you gonna go and hole up 'til you got your strength back?"

Bear shrugs, takes his smoking pipe from his pocket, fidgets with it and packs some loose tobacco into the bowl. Blowing the flakes, he mutters, "I ain't thought that far ahead. Figured I'd just drift a bit, maybe head back toward Texas."

Looking over to Alice standing with her belongings, Holton inquires, "And, where do you plan on drifting?"

Distraught, she stares at Holton. "I thought maybe I could get some sort of work in Prescott."

"If work is what you're lookin' for, there is plenty of that for you here, and free room and board to boot."

Bear grunts, "That's sure not what I'm lookin' for…"

Alice adds, "I don't want to be where I'm not wanted."

Her comment evokes the response she had intended, and Holton stands to face her. As he stares at her, Bear averts his gaze, lights his pipe and takes a few puffs. Holton states, "Alice… You're wanted here."

She flushes with relief, smiles, and asks demurely. "You need me to stay?"

Holton steps to her and reaches his hands out to place them on the sides of her arms. "No, I don't *need* you to stay. But, I want you to stick around."

Between smoking puffs on his pipe, Bear murmurs, "Don't sugar-coat it too much for her, pard."

After glancing over at Bear, Alice looks back to Holton. She thinks on what he said for a moment, and she then stares out at the view of the faraway hills. "I don't want to continue staying if there isn't a future in it."

Above the Llano

Holton leans in, gives her a kiss and speaks tenderly. "You never know what the future might hold for anyone... But, I'd really like it if you'd stay on here a while longer."

She moves into his open arms and, with another touch of their lips, they embrace. Behind, Bear coughs his throat clear, gets up from his chair and gingerly scoots around them. "Well, I guess I had better get my gear and be going."

They both turn to Bear, and Alice is first to speak. "Please, Bear... You don't have to go."

Holton nods his agreement. "At least stay here a spell, until you're full healed."

Scratching behind his ear with the stem of his pipe, Bear shakes his head, unsure. "I don't want to interfere with yer buddin' courtship none."

Holton glances out to the barn and a stand of trees not far beyond the wood-chopping pile. "How about we build you a cabin?"

Bear looks at Holton quizzically. "Ya mean a home? Permanent-like...?"

"Yeah, something for you to stay in when you're here. You ain't getting any younger, and, these days, the military is just a bunch of cadet school kids."

The old scout sucks at his pipe and ponders this option. An idea forms, and there is a twinkle in his eye as he blows out a cloud of smoke. Clenching the pipe stem in his teeth, he comments, "Ever since I've knowed him, I've always bin kinda partial to stayin' at Charlie's cabin."

Holton is confused, until Alice grips him tighter around the middle. Holding him close, she states, "I would sure like a cabin of our own and to share a home with you."

As a chill of realization comes over Holton, he needs a moment to sort out his mixed feelings. Alice and Bear wait while the state of affairs shapes up for him. Looking inside the old, dilapidated, bachelor cabin and then down at Alice's arms wrapped lovingly around him, he surmises, "You're probably gonna want a bigger cabin than Bear was gonna need…"

She smiles sweetly at him. "Could be there is an addition to the family someday…"

Bear grunts and takes the pipe from his mouth. "Holton, for a lone oak, you sure do spread some wide roots."

Flustered, Holton shakes his head at his old friend. "I'm not exactly sure how I agreed to all this. I was just trying to make you both feel welcome." Holton looks down at Alice, back to Bear, and then hesitantly bends down to give her a soft peck on the forehead.

Chapter 27

The Comanche have regrouped in quick order. The main campfire has died down considerably, and nearly all of the escaped hostages have been rounded up and restrained again. The captives' situation hasn't improved as they are back near the spring-fed pond, guarded by several attentive braves.

Clustered with the others, Jules tugs at his tightly bound hands and touches the tender lump on his forehead. Blinking his eyes to chase away the throbbing pain in his head, he looks down at his empty holster and knife sheath. The stars shine brighter, as the campfires dies down and Jules' eyes adjust to the night.

At the pony herd, the warriors mount up and prepare to depart. Jules watches, as a Comanche brave comes over and starts to pull each of the captives to their feet. A whimpering yelp from an adolescent boy catches everyone's attention, and they watch him hunker on the ground, refusing to stand up. The warrior attempts to pull him to his feet, barks some harsh words at the boy, and then violently kicks him repeatedly with the toe of his moccasin. The boy continues to sob, but still refuses to comply.

Restricted by his bindings, Jules whispers loudly as he struggles to stand. "Get up, boy... We'll be rescued soon!"

The Comanche turns to briefly glare at Jules, before taking his knife from its sheath and slicing the blade across the recalcitrant youth's throat. The whimper of protest turns to a gurgling cough, and the captive boy dies an agonizing death. The remaining prisoners obey and cling closer together, as the Comanche takes a step forward to assess Jules.

The warrior gives a harsh glare that seems to pierce right through, but Jules stands up straight and remains stoic. In fragmented English, the Comanche hisses, "No devil-rangers come for you." The warrior sheathes his bloody knife and takes up a length of rope that binds the captives together. He tosses it up to a brave on horseback and heads to the pony herd to grab his own mount.

Jules turns to cast his gaze up the rocky bluff, hoping to see his ranger friends, with their rifles, perched high above. Instead, only the faintest light of morning greets him above the steep, vacant wall. He hears a sound in the underbrush, and thinks he might see the eyes of Dog staring back at him. As the Indians begin to move out, the tether line is pulled to lead the captives away. Jules lets out a sharp whistle and hollers toward the brush, "Dog... Go get help!"

The Comanche holding the lead rope jerks the line, as he prods his horse forward. Another horseback warrior draws back his bow and aims. Jules calls out again, "Go, Dog!" before being silenced by the stinging whack of a leather quirt. When the warrior releases the arrow into the bushes, something moves back and rushes away.

~*~

Up the hillside, just a short distance from the original ranch cabin, Holton and Bear clear rocks from the build site. They carefully stack the gathered stones around the perimeter

112

to create a rudimentary foundation. Breathing heavily, Bear takes a rest on a boulder and wipes the sweat from his brow. While he catches his breath, he gets out his pipe and scrapes the tobacco residue from inside the bowl. His gaze travels over to where his friend is still working, and he remarks, "This is more work than I think I signed on for."

In a sweat-soaked shirt, Holton carries a large rock and sets it by the others. "You need the activity to get you well."

"I may need a doctor's opinion on that one."

Holton stands straight and stretches his back muscles. He wipes the sweat dripping down his cheek, and grumbles. "If you would have just left well enough alone, we'd only be making you a new cabin not near this size."

Sucking on his empty pipe, the cavalry scout nods. "Durn'it… Figures it would be a woman that makes us prove-up this place."

Looking around, Holton nods his agreement. "Yeah… Ol' Charlie wasn't really one for airs nor upkeep."

The empty pipe whistles softly and Bear looks down the grade to the ramshackle cabin. "Ya know, Holton, I think she might of tricked us somehow…"

Holton adjusts his sweated hat and lowers his chin. "The thing about having a woman around the place is that she gets you to thinkin' what *she* wants is what *you* really want."

Laughing, Bear adds, "More-so when they's pretty."

"She do get the blood to rise."

Bear chews on the stem of his smoking pipe, as he gazes down to the trees near the pasture and horse corrals. "How about I take the wagon into town and trade some of them beeves for a load of cut lumber?"

With a flat shovel, Holton scoops aside a load of dirt. "Yer not just wanting to visit the saloon a spell?"

"We are gettin' a bit short on medicinal supplies."

"Fine by me."

Bear packs tobacco in his pipe, and then grins when he sees Alice come from the cabin and wave them in for a meal. He wipes his palm on his leg, tucks the pipe away and grunts. "Hmm. Maybe I'll spend a night or two…"

Holton grins perceptively and asks, "You hungry?"

"Yeah, for more'n jest whiskey…"

~*~

Dog trots toward the horizon, first at a limp, then slowly picking up the pace until he is running nearly full out. As day transitions into night, the canine travels ever westward at an even, loping pace …

Chapter 28

It has been several days of difficult travel, on foot, through the hill country. Jules and the others, beat-down and tired, offer no resistance when left in camp under a lone sentinel. Later, a war party returns with fresh scalps hanging across saddle blankets and newly acquired hostages in tow.

Despondent, Jules can't help but think back on what his sisters must have gone through at the hands of Bloody Ben and his outlaw gang. Mentally detached, he retreats, choosing not to engage with the other captives. His internal turmoil haunts him, and he becomes emotionless. As the days pass, Jules withdraws further and further until he becomes just a shell of the person he was.

~*~

The band of Comanche leads their prisoners through a rock-strewn gulch and stop at a cavernous hole in the ground. A twisting, water-cut path descends downward to a series of underground caves. Several natives emerge to exchange words with the arriving war party. The casual conversation turns to animated excitement, as the Comanche relate tales of pillaging and capture.

A nervous murmur travels amongst the group of captives, as some at the front of the group peer down into the narrow opening. Cool, dank air rises from the rocky hollow, carrying with it an odorous mix of bat guano, fire and sweat. One of the prisoners looks behind to Jules and nervously asks, "Where do you think they're taking us?"

Jules peers down at the entrance of the cavern to see the glowing reflection of a campfire on the inner wall. He looks at the long line of captives behind him and the vast expanse beyond, devoid of any hint of rescue. He despondently utters, "Into hell, I suppose…"

~*~

The wagonload of lumber is pulled up alongside the site for the new cabin. A stone foundation has been built up, and there is now a floor with its walls beginning to be erected. The makings of a stone fireplace stand at the wall opposite the main entry and porch.

Sweating under the noon sun, Holton works shirtless. He looks over to where Bear, with a clay jug of moonshine, sits in the shade of a tree. Taking a break, Holton suggests, "Save some of that for me, will ya?"

Bear belches under his breath and points toward a stick of lumber, as Holton lifts it to fasten to another part of the cabin. "Make sure that wall is straight now, or she'll nag you and never let you hear the end of it."

Grimacing, Holton finishes hammering the piece in place and puts his tool aside. He wipes sweat from his temple, adjusts his hat, and reaches out for the jug as he walks over to Bear, "You're a hell of a one to give me directions on anything being on the straight and narrow."

Grinning, Bear hands up the jug. "I have me a system."

"What's that?"

"I kin drink jest enough, so when an object blurs into threes, I can jest concentrate on the one in the middle."

Holton shakes his head and takes a swig from the jug. "Keep on drinking this stuff like you are, and you'll be blind b'fore you see the bottom." He takes a seat next to Bear and sets the jug down between them. A warm breeze blows past, as they silently admire the weeks' work.

Leaning back on the tree, Bear nods his approval. "Well, it's comin' together."

"Without much help from you..."

Putting on a drunken smile, Bear modestly protests. "Well, I do my best to stay out of the way." From afar, a croaking bark travels in on the breeze, Both Holton and Bear turn to face the source of the sound. Bear gives a chuckle. "Damned if that don't remind me of a friend of your'n..."

A tingling of gooseflesh travels down both his arms at the thought of the loyal canine, and Holton nods his head. "He was a good dog."

"All this sittin' around business kinda makes me miss that trooper of a kid, too."

"Yeah..." Holton stares off into the distance, listening. He doesn't hear or see anything that might resemble his old canine companion or the boy he felt responsible to look after.

Bear reminisces, as he observes Holton lost in thought. "Gee, that kid... He sure had some muddled thoughts when he went off with them Texas Rangers."

"Yep."

The two sit quietly a moment, until Bear speaks again. "Ya think he'll ever catch up with that Bloody Ben character?"

"Nope."

Bear sits up to look curiously at Holton. "Why not? Heck, I'd put my money on 'im. He was pretty determined."

Pulling his gaze from the horizon, Holton looks at Bear before lifting the jug for another swallow. Feeling the home-brew burn through his innards, he winces as he responds. "'Cause I found that outlaw holed-up along the river a day or two later... He was none to good for lastin'."

"Ya finish 'im?"

Holton sighs, as he looks out to the far ridgeline again. "He was near-finished already from what the boy had done."

"You ever think to tell that kid about it?"

After thinking a moment, Holton shakes his head. "Don't think it would've made much of a difference anyhow. Grief has a way of washing away the bitter taste for revenge."

Suddenly, with a yelping bark, a running dog emerges over the distant hillside. As the scruffy canine approaches, Bear blinks and rubs his eyes. "I'll be danged, if'n that ain't yer mangy, ol' mongrel!" As Dog bounds into the valley and lopes toward them, Holton smiles, stands and whistles. Incredulous, Bear glances at his jug of moonshine and then back to the dog. "Damn! I don't believe my eyes..."

"Why's that?"

"Cause there's three of 'em!"

Chapter 29

On the cabin porch, Dog rests, listening to the activity inside. He raises his head and leans back to lick at his thigh wound, and then sits up as Holton comes out the door with a set of saddlebags and his big-loop rifle. The man looks down at the dog and they exchange a silent but familiar understanding.

Following Holton out to the porch, Alice, visibly upset, declares, "I don't understand... How you could know that?"

Bear appears in the doorway behind Alice, as Holton turns to address her. "I just do... I can't explain it, but me and Dog here have had us an understanding for a long time."

Exasperated, Alice pivots to Bear in the doorway, and then back to Holton. "You told that dog to stay with the boy, so now you think he's in trouble because the dog is here?"

Holton glances down at Dog and ponders the thought. "That's about the jist of it..."

"That's ridiculous!" She looks to Bear for support. "What do you have to say?" When he doesn't respond straightaway, she barks at him. "Anything?!?"

Sheepishly, Bear meets her stern glare and then shrugs. "He is a funny kinda dog that way." Dog lifts up his head, fixes his dark eyes on Bear and lets out a rumbling growl.

Frowning, Bear shakes his head. "Over the years, I've seen him do some mighty unexpected things."

Alice stares hard at Bear. Then, she sniffs and catches a whiff of the alcohol on his breath. "You're drunk!"

"Yes, ma'am."

Holton tilts his head, gesturing for Dog to follow him, and steps down from the porch with his rifle and saddlebags. "I won't be but a month or so, there and back."

In disbelief, Alice stares at him from the top step of the porch stairs. "What about finishing our cabin?"

"Bear can do it."

"Huh?" Suddenly strong in opinion, Bear announces, "The hell I am. I'm going with you!"

Holton thinks about Bear's bandaged wound that is still on the mend. "You ain't healed well enough for the trip. You'll only slow me down."

Bear protests. "I ain't staying here."

"You brought her here yerself, so you can watch over her while I'm gone."

Bear considers the sobering argument, as he stumbles down the stairs and hustles up alongside Holton. Tentatively, he glances back at Alice as he whispers, "I don't think I should be left alone with a proper woman."

Astounded, Holton remarks, "You didn't seem to feel that way when you brought her here in the first place."

Looking over his shoulder toward Alice again, Bear lowers his voice even more. "Heck, I was jest going to leave her with you and skedaddle."

Holton smiles facetiously and gives Bear a pat on the shoulder. "Funny how things work out..."

"Not really..."

"Rest yourself awhile and keep healin' on yer wound. Work on that cabin, and I'll be back shortly." Holton proceeds to the barn to gather his saddle gear, with Bear on his heels hoping to change his mind.

As Holton swings the barn door open, Bear stops. Fumbling to find the appropriate words, he finally proclaims, "She'll try to civilize me!!!"

Laughing, Holton exits with his saddle and tosses it over the top rail of the corral. "There are worse things a woman could do to ya…"

Bear sputters, "Holton, if you go 'n leave me here with an angry woman… And git yerself killed, or don't come back. I'll never forgive you."

Turning to look at his friend, Holton nods in reply. "Fair enough…"

Dog comes along to join them and Bear looks down at the mutt. "Damn you, ya cur-hound." Sitting on his haunches, the dog looks up at Bear, curls back his lips and gives a snarl. The cavalry scout takes a cautious step back and spits aside. He watches Holton enter the corral to grab his horse and then looks back at Dog. "Why didn't you jest stick with that boy like we asked?"

~*~

The captives are led through a series of water-worn caves and tunnels. In one large grotto, a group of Indians lazing around a campfire watch them file by. Other niches contain random piles of loot from recent raids. Jules notices the glint of a steel blade near some bolts of cloth and a discarded pile of settler clothing. He stumbles a few steps and falls to his knees on the hard stone floor. The sudden tug of the lead line causes the whole line of captives to cluster together and crowd around him.

The brave at the head of the group comes back to assess the problem. Angrily, he growls, "Get up, lazy white-eye…" Swiftly, Jules reaches to grab the knife, hiding it in his hand.

He conceals the blade at his side, as he rises to his feet. Striking out with a riding quirt made from the foot of a deer, the Comanche curses, and the sharp sting causes Jules to flinch away and tuck his head in defense. In his native tongue, the Comanche continues to berate the boy. "You cower like a woman under the whip!"

His gaze lowered at the ground to avoid any further confrontation, Jules doesn't respond. Another hard smack of the leather quirt strikes him across the shoulder blade, and he quickly resumes his position in the single-file line of captives. The Comanche stares at Jules for a moment, and then, for good measure, gives him one more whack with the rawhide. With a tug of the lead rope, the prisoners continue through the maze of underground chambers.

Chapter 30

Holton puts a boot to the stirrup, mounts his horse, looks down at the mangy dog, and then looks over to Bear. The two men exchange a look that reflects a long and trusted friendship. He then glances to the cabin porch, where Alice stands watching them. Nudging his horse, he guides it toward the cabin, with Dog sauntering along at the gelding's heels. Holton leans down over the saddle horn, until he is about eye level with Alice. He pushes his hat to the back of his head and wipes his brow. They quietly stare at each other for a moment, until Holton finally states, "I'll be back in a month or so..."

"I might not still be here when you return."

Holton purses his lips with acceptance and replies. "There is always that chance..." She realizes that her womanly threats have had little effect on the independent-minded westerner and quickly changes her tactics. "Please, don't go."

"That boy might be needin' my help."

Alice casts a look down at the canine and remarks, "Maybe he just sent the dog away." Dog sits his injured haunches on the ground and lets out a low, rumbling growl.

Holton quiets the dog with a look. "Alice, I hoped you would understand. Ya see, I don't have any kinfolk, and that boy is the closest thing to it."

"What about me?"

"You're here and safe."

"What if I leave?"

Holton takes a breath and ponders her statement. "Women have to do that sometimes. Nothing I do or don't do is gonna make much of a difference."

"Maybe it will."

Holton lowers his gaze and shakes his head unhappily. "If not this time, it'll be another. It's best to do what needs doing and avoid the regret."

Desperate, Alice pleads with Holton. "You would lose me over a *hunch* that the boy needs you, because of a gesture from a *dog*?!?"

"I generally let folks do what they want to do and don't judge them for that."

Recognizing that she can't convince him to change his plans, she drops her gaze and then looks over toward Bear near the corrals. "Goodbye, Holton..."

He nods solemnly. "Alice, I'll be back soon enough." She continues to stare off into the distance... away from him. He looks down at the dog, sighs, and gives a soft whistle. "C'mon Dog." Turning his mount from the cabin, Holton touches his spurs to the horse's flank. Followed by the canine, he travels down the ranch lane.

Left standing on the porch, Alice turns her gaze to watch him go. She bows her head and then goes back into the cabin. At the corrals, Bear lifts an open hand skyward and holds it there until Holton and Dog finally pass from sight. "Safe journeys, my friend..."

~*~

Gathered with other captives in the musty chamber, they all sit staring at one another. A small fire, tended-to by a warrior armed with a rifle, crackles at the cavern's entrance.

Above the Llano

The prisoners talk quietly amongst themselves, until the Comanche grunts to hush them. During a long stretch of silence, Jules, listening to the crackle of the campfire, starts to hear a discreet whisper traveling among the captives again.

Carefully, he takes the concealed knife from his sleeve and steadies the handle of the blade upright between his heels. Slow and deliberate, he cuts at the rawhide bindings wrapped around his wrists. At first, the twists of leather seem impenetrable, but then they start to give way as the knife edge cuts through the fibers. Patiently, the boy presses his bindings against the metal with a firm pushing and pulling motion.

Two more Indians come into the cave holding a lantern. They walk among the seated captives and jerk one of the teenage girls to her feet. Another woman jumps up to try and stop them, but she is violently knocked to the cavern floor. Maliciously, the captors repeatedly kick and punch the woman, until her protesting screams reduce to a whimper.

They laugh, as she lies curled in a submissive ball. After exchanging a series of low, guttural words with the guard, they then exit the cavern, dragging the terrified girl as she sobs and tries to squirm free. The cavern is left to the sounds of the crackling fire and the muffled cries of the woman huddled on the floor. Quietly, Jules resumes the laborious task of cutting at the leather ties around his wrists.

~*~

Under a starry night sky, Holton sits staring into the jumping flames of a small campfire. With the light glowing on his features, he looks over at the loyal canine sitting nearby. Dog crinkles his brow, gazing up to his longtime companion. Holton frowns. "Why are you looking at me like that?"

Dog blinks and lowers his chin to his front paws. Sighing, Holton casts his gaze to the surrounding darkness. "Dog... It *is* good to see you again, but the conversations sure

125

haven't gotten any better." The canine snorts, blowing his nose into the dusty ground and, with dark, twinkling eyes, stares up at Holton. He looks at Dog and somberly comments, "I sure do miss that kid…"

The dog lets out a small whine and then turns to lick at the recent wound on his hip. Holton nods in response. "Yeah… I hope he's all right too." The fire slowly dies down to a whispering crackle, while evening stars light up the cloudless heavens above.

Chapter 31

Jules sits among the younger captives, and he eyes each one of them carefully. Unsure of who might have enough spirit and strength to attempt an escape, he keeps the news of the stolen knife and his unbound hands to himself. He listens, as the sounds of the whimpering woman slowly fade to an occasional sniffling.

The flicker of firelight allows Jules to make out the figure of a young boy seated next to the defeated form of the protective mother. At the only entrance to the cavern, the fire has nearly burned down to embers, and adds a smoky haze to the already dank air. The lone guard appears to be sleeping, with his rifle cradled across his chest and head canted back.

Without a clear plan of escape, Jules considers the possibility of fleeing alone. Or, perhaps, he could attempt to free all of the hostages, which would probably get a lot of them killed. He observes that a few captives still have a bit of life in them, while others have accepted their grim fate and slipped into oblivion. He carefully weighs the consequences, as he sits and waits for an opportunity.

~*~

Traveling east toward Texas, Holton rides steadily through the Chihuahan desert. Trotting ahead, following an unseen path to the boy, Dog occasionally disappears into the underbrush. Focused on the horizon, Holton reflects on the familiar southwestern landscapes. His mind drifts to thoughts of life with the Apache, his young Indian wife, and then, finally, to the woman he left behind at the ranch.

The vibrant memories of his fighting days and his youthful quest for adventure lead him to more recent memories of his time with Jules and searching for the boy's stolen sisters. As the miles gradually pass away under his horse's footfalls, Holton has ample time to reflect and consider the choices made on his journey through life.

~*~

While he loses track of days and nights in the hollow depths, Jules' eyes gradually become more accustomed to the constant dimness. Noticing details that were once cloaked in shadow, he is able to identify narrow crevices along the walls. The campfire at the entrance serves as a consistent source of light and proves to be the only deterrent from total darkness.

A small group of Comanche braves enter the cavern and, with a blunt kick, gruffly wake the snoozing sentinel. One of the braves drops an armload of firewood, while another places a few sticks over the glowing embers. As the fire builds up, Jules crawls closer to the conversing Indians. The Comanche dialogue is peppered with small bits of Spanish and English, but all he can make out is: *war party... above the Llano...* and *when the fire goes out...*

Jules scoots back slowly to keep from the reach of the growing firelight and discovers a small fracture in the wall. His fingers probe the crumbling rock, and he finds a narrow, water-worn gap. Extending his arm into the fissure, he feels around and finds that it widens just past the narrow opening.

Above the Llano

Careful not to let anyone see him, Jules slips through the crack in the wall. He scoots in as far back as he can fit, and finds that he is able to stand.

Completely hidden from the light of the campfire, Jules is unable to squeeze any further through the narrow opening. Disappointed that this is not an exit to use as a means of escape, Jules slides out of the crevice and moves back to his seated position along the wall. Looking at the silent captives with their heads lowered in defeat, he notices the eyes of the young boy by the woman, watching him in the darkness.

~*~

Holton rides through rolling, tree-scattered landscape. The only shade from the hot sun comes from oaks that spread their long limbs over scrubby tufts of grass, wildflowers and brush. Ahead, Dog climbs a perch of boulders and gazes northward to where the terrain rises into a rocky dome. Bringing his mount up beside the canine, Holton looks over at the dog as if he could hear him speak, and then follows the animal's lingering stare. He asks aloud, "We gettin' near...?" Dog lets out a bark, leaps from the rocks and trots through the valley toward the higher elevations beyond. Holton prods his horse onward and follows.

Chapter 32

Dog scampers up the dome of rock and stops to look back at Holton coming behind. He drops to his haunches, pants with his tongue out, and waits. The horse's hooves softly clomp on the gritty stone, as they steadily make their way uphill.

After following the dog's lead up the steep grade, Holton halts his mount and looks down to where Dog sits. Dried blood smears the rocks and tells of an injured person recently being carried off. "Yeah, I see it Dog..." Holton nods his head, and the dog trots forward toward a slick rock clearing on higher ground that leads to a group of boulders.

Holton crests the high ridge and cautiously approaches the circle of larger rocks. He pins his ears back in case his scouting companion decides to warn him of hidden danger. Coming around the rocks, he encounters the decayed carcass of a horse beside a pile of stones that marks a recent grave. After scanning the area, Holton appreciates the vantage over the lower terrain. He dismounts, squats into a defensive position and notices the shell casings scattered all around. "Good spot to hole up and hold out..."

He takes note of the smattering of arrows and items of saddle gear that were left behind after the engagement. Playing out the series of events in his mind, Holton moves to each rock-sheltered position. "After a day or two here, they must've decided to move out for water and supplies..."

Dog sits in the shade of a scrubby cedar, gazing at the scattered pieces of horse hair and bone. Then, lying down and putting his head to his paws, he lets his eyes follow the man. Holton walks over to the dog and notices a flint-tipped arrow shaft lying nearby. Intuitively understanding the dog's mood, he muses, "Caught one of those, did ya?"

~*~

At the cavern entrance, the guard uses the last of his wood supply to build up the fire. The sound of warriors approaching creates a nervous tension among the captives. With a keen sense that something bad is about to happen, Jules keeps to the shadows and pushes back to the wall.

As the group outside nears, the rattling clank of a chain dragging across the rock floor can be heard. Jules peers at the dimly-lit crowd of captives, trying to spot the young boy next to the woman. The mass of huddled forms shifts anxiously, and the sound of the jingling chain echoes louder, until it finally stops near the entrance.

Jules stealthily scoots up against the wall and tucks himself into the narrow crevice. At the back of the constricted space, he is startled when he suddenly bumps into someone. When he puts his hand out to feel, Jules quickly realizes that this must be the young boy that was intently watching him earlier. Pressed firmly against the boy, Jules faintly murmurs, "What are you doing in here?"

In a hushed, timid voice, the younger boy answers, "They're going to kill us all, aren't they?"

Jules tries to make out the features of the boy but can't see any details in the total darkness. "Give me your hands." The boy blindly pushes his bound hands out in front of him, and Jules uses the knife to cut through the rawhide bindings. He whispers to the boy. "Stay here with me."

"Are you a Texas Ranger?"

"No, but some will come for us." As shouts of urgency and pleas of mercy echo through the chamber, Jules shields the boy by pressing him further toward the back of the space. The sound of chains clanking, and of children crying as they are shackled, fills Jules with dread.

Whimpering, the little boy puts his hands to his ears. "What's going on?!?"

Jules hugs the boy's head tightly, trying to block out the sounds of the captives being rounded-up. "Shhh… Shush… Quiet now or they'll find us."

Several long, agonizing minutes pass… Jules can only imagine the terrible fate of the homesteaders being led out of the cave by a rusty length of chain.

~*~

Holton rides north from the domed rock formation. Alert in the saddle, he keeps his big-loop rifle cocked and ready, positioned across his lap. Observing the stalking dog, he follows the trusted canine as the animal keeps his nose to the ground picking up the trail of the departed rangers.

Chapter 33

At the creek crossing, Holton holds his mount and listens. His ears perk to the sound of trickling water, insects in the grass, birds in the trees, and the leaves shifting in the breeze. He swings a leg over the saddle, dismounts, and kneels down. Studying the trail, he sees that the group of riders they follow split ranks before crossing.

With his rifle across his lap, Holton squats beside the creek and slowly scans the area. Playing the scenario out in his mind, he looks to both sides of the stream, taking note of the trampled grass and shoreline erosion. He murmurs to the dog. "Good place to set up an ambush..."

~*~

In the concealing darkness of the crevice, Jules hugs the boy close to him and looks out toward the smoldering fire. There is a haze of smoke in the air and, now that the captives have been ushered away, complete stillness in the cavern. Jules releases his embrace of the child and eases toward the crevice opening. He motions to stop, and whispers to the boy. "Stay put a minute..."

Poking his head out, Jules looks out into the dark cavern and notices a curled-up body, unmoving, on the floor. Jules waits and listens. After determining that everyone is gone and not coming back, he slides back into the crevice and takes the young boy by the hand. "They're gone. Let's go."

The boy follows Jules out of the crack in the wall and into the cavern. As they move toward the chamber's entrance, the young boy stops to linger beside the huddled figure lying still on the ground. The boy drops to his knees and whimpers a sorrowful moan. Jules hesitates, and assumes the worst. "C'mon kid, we have to go."

The sound of nearing footsteps attracts Jules' attention. He jumps to the side and flattens himself against the wall. To no avail, he hisses at the crying boy. "Kid! Come over here…"

At the entrance to the large cavern, an Indian appears near the campfire embers and he stares into the obscure void. He makes a clucking sound with his tongue, when he spots the figure hunched over the body. In Comanche, he calls, "Come here, you!" The brave moves into the cave and grabs the young boy by the collar.

After pulling him to his feet and whacking him hard with the back of his hand, he drags the squirming youth to the exit. As they pass through the light of the smoldering fire, Jules watches but holds back. The boy desperately looks around in a silent plea for aid, but none comes. Suddenly, Jules dashes from the shadows, leaps at the Comanche and plunges his blade into his neck. The Indian struggles, gurgles a dying protest then crumples to the ground and lies still.

"C'mon, we have to go!" Jules reaches his hand out to the boy, but the young child rushes back to the body in the center of the cavern. Jules hurries over to the boy and pulls him back to his feet. He looks down at the dead woman and grimly utters, "Do you know that person?"

The sniffling child casts a teary gaze up at Jules. "Sh…she's my Mama."

Above the Llano

Swallowing the lump that rises in his throat, Jules musters the courage to speak. "I'm really sorry about her... But, we must go now." The child wipes away his tears and grabs hold of Jules' outstretched hand. In the hope of escape, they leave the dead behind and make their way into the dark passageway.

~*~

The sun shines brightly, as Holton rides up to the location of the war-party campsite below the rocky bluff. Idling by the pool of fresh water, he lets his horse lower its head to drink and surveys the location. Satisfied that no one is around, he dismounts and walks over to the remains of a fire.

Slowly walking around, Holton identifies where the pony herd was kept. He then moves to the other side of the pond where the grassy vegetation still remains flattened by a group of people that were clustered there. He softly murmurs, "There were more than a few captives... Where are you, boy?" Holton stops to quietly think for a moment. "Was it you back there under them grave stones?" From the nearby bushes, Dog barks to get his attention. Holton cautiously looks around. After one last check of the campsite, he goes to see what the canine has found.

In the dirt under a bush lies a firearm with an ivory handle. Holton takes a knee, reaches into the brush and pulls out the engraved pistol that was once carried by Jules. Weighing the short-barreled handgun in his palm, he muses, "I remember taking this and giving it to the boy."

Gazing around the site, Holton sees scattered tracks of several men and the dragging heel marks of a pair of boots. Exchanging a perceptive expression with Dog, he can't help but mention aloud, "If they drug him off, then he was probably still alive."

The dog whimpers, puts his nose to the ground and trots off to the location where the captives were once held. Holton returns to the campsite and tucks the engraved pistol in his saddlebag. While he stands ruminating about the possible sequence of events, he suddenly hears a low, rumbling growl. The canine stands focused on the thick brush, just outside the camp. Holton clutches his rifle and slowly cocks back the hammer.

Chapter 34

There is a rustling in the mesquite, and two men horseback suddenly appear. As Holton pivots to face them, he brings his rifle to his shoulder and takes aim. A familiar voice calls out. "Hold it! Don't shoot..."

Holton stares directly down the rifle sights toward a man that he only vaguely recognizes. Finger on the trigger, Holton replies, "Don't give me a reason."

Surprisingly, the dog appears at the fringe of the brush, looks to Ranger Bentley and lets out an acknowledging bark. The ranger captain glances to the canine and looks over to where Holton still aims his rifle. "Easy now, I know that dog. And, I know you."

Holton's mind races through the many faces he's seen in the past few years. Finally, he lowers this rifle and suggests, "Step down from there and tell me about it."

Raising his right hand up and away from his sidearm, Ranger Bentley swings his leg over his mount to step down. He looks at the mounted ranger beside him and gives a nod. "It's okay, McCandles... This here is a friend of Jules Ward." Sliding to the ground, Bentley returns his attention to Holton. "Mister Lang, is it?"

"That's right."

"How exactly did you come to be here?"

139

"Dog came for me."

Ranger Bentley can't help but crack a smile, as he glances over at the dog. He peers back to the business end of Holton's rifle and warily comments, "The last time we met, you were after Bloody Ben, and then you were heading to a ranch west of here." With the clear memory of a graveside conversation before saying goodbye to Jules, Holton remembers why he knows the man. The ranger continues. "Arizona, I believe?"

"Where's the boy?"

"That's what we're trailing after to find out."

Still cautious, Holton looks up to Corky, and then back to Bentley. "Tell your man to step down, and we'll talk."

The ranger captain gestures to Corky McCandles. "Climb down like he said." In disbelief, the mounted ranger looks at the dog and then back to the buckskin-clad man with the unique rifle. He steps down from the saddle and stands by his horse. Ranger Bentley hands over his reins to his subordinate and takes a step toward Holton, who still holds his rifle at the ready.

"You always keep one in the chamber?"

"Only when I'm carrying it."

As Bentley approaches, Holton carefully lets down the rifle's hammer. Over his shoulder, the ranger gestures to the brush, commenting, "We were watching you from afar, and, when no one else joined you, figured we'd have a closer look."

Intrigued, Holton raises an eyebrow and responds, "They only send out two rangers after a group of raiding Comanche as large as this?"

Bentley nods his head, as he looks around at the now-abandoned Indian camp. "We were several more in numbers a few weeks ago. Some were killed, and I sent two others toward Mason to raise up more men to join us."

Above the Llano

Letting his gaze travel to the spot where the cluster of hostages was kept, Holton comments. "They took captives..."

"Yes, we know."

"Is Jules among them?"

Bentley nods solemnly. "We haven't found a body yet, so we assume he is."

Reaching over his saddle, Holton slips his rifle back into the scabbard. He gathers the reins, puts his foot to the stirrup and mounts. The rangers look up to him, and Bentley asks, "Where are you going?"

"After the boy..."

The captain looks to the ranger behind him and then scans the vacant camp. "Just *you*? *Alone*...?"

Turning his horse, Holton gives a low whistle to Dog. "A man who journeys out alone ought to know he can handle himself before setting off."

Staring up at the horseback westerner, Corky exclaims, "But, there are more than a few dozen of them Indians!"

"Yer both welcome to tag along, if'n you don't bother me none."

Snuffling at the roundabout insult, Ranger Bentley peers up at Holton. "I assure you, Mister Lang, we won't get in your way, and, if you're only just after the boy, you won't be in ours."

When Holton tilts his head, Dog trots off away from the camp. He nudges his horse to follow and calls out behind him, "Come along, then. The day's a wastin'."

Bentley returns to his horse and takes up the reins. Corky watches Holton ride away after the dog and utters, "Who is that guy?"

"That's Holton Lang."

Confused, Corky crinkles his brow. "Am I supposed to know who that is?"

141

Ranger Bentley slips his foot in the stirrup and throws a leg over his saddle. "Nope... I can't imagine why you would, but, once you do, you'll never forget."

~*~

Inside the dark underground passageways, Jules leads the young boy to the best of his ability. Feeling their hands along the cold, damp walls, they make their way. Up ahead, they see the faint glow of a campfire flickering off the slick stone walls and head toward it.

At the end to the side tunnel, just beyond the firelight, Jules thinks he might see a way out. Not willing to take the gamble of being discovered or recaptured, he hesitates. Twice, he pulls the boy back, and they flatten themselves against the cave wall as warriors rush past.

The boy whispers, "Where are they going?"

"Looks to be everyone is leaving this place in a hurry. Maybe the rangers tracked us here and found the entrance..."

"We're to be rescued?"

Jules watches until the path is clear and then leads the boy on. "We have to rescue ourselves." Sticking together, trying their best to avoid capture while searching for an alternate exit, they continue feeling their way through the dark, unmarked tunnels.

Chapter 35

From the cover of bushes, Holton, Bentley and Corky observe the Comanche warriors gathering at the entrance of the cave. The Indians pack up their bounty and load it onto sleds and travois for transport. Holton glances beside at the rangers. "Looks like they'll be moving out soon."

Bentley lifts a set of field glasses to his eyes and notes, "They have been raiding down south for months and are now probably headed to the panhandle for the rest of the season."

Corky has to start over when taking a headcount, as Comanche warriors pour out of the cave like bees from a hive. "I can't count them quick enough. They jest keep coming out of the ground."

Watching the war party assemble, Holton and Bentley each silently formulate their own plans. When Bentley lowers his field glasses, Holton asks, "Do you see the boy there?"

"Not yet…"

"Then, I'll have to go in and get him."

Taken aback at the notion, Bentley turns to Holton. "How would you ever get inside?"

Holton narrows his eyes to study the terrain around the cave entrance. "These underground hollows were formed by rivers passing through them a long time ago. I ain't seen a water flow yet that won't change directions from where it's supposed to..."

"You think there is another way in?"

"If there is, I'll find it."

All of a sudden, a tormented, communal wail, accompanied by the rattling of chains, erupts from the mouth of the cave. Attentive, the three men watch from concealment, as the restrained captives are led out. Shielding their eyes from the intense daylight, the unkempt prisoners react with fear and confusion. When an anguished prisoner screams out, a warrior swings a club and knocks her to the ground. As she continues to wail, the Comanche clubs her repeatedly, until, finally, she falls quiet. Clinging to their chains, the remaining captives huddle together for security.

From his hiding spot, Corky takes aim with his rifle. "Just say the word, Cap'n, and I'll kill that son-of-a-bitch."

Shaking his head, Bentley puts his hand out to lower the barrel of Corky's rifle. "Hold your fire. If we start in on them now, they'll surely kill the hostages and be all over us. No one will be any better off."

Holton narrows his gaze, trying to identify the captives. "What was the boy wearing?"

Ranger Bentley studies the prisoners, looking for Jules. "I don't see him down there... But, it's hard to tell."

Holton nods, and looks behind to see Dog watching. "I'm gonna find another way inside there."

The ranger captain turns and glances at Holton again. "Hold it, Lang... Those, right there, are probably all of the live hostages. We need to concentrate our efforts on the whole. Not just one that we don't even know is still alive..."

The westerner tilts his head toward the captives. "That's your job, Captain. You go on and do it. If Jules is alive,

I'll find 'im and do mine." Bentley clenches his jaw taut, as he watches Holton make his way back to the horses.

Corky sights his rifle on the Indians below. "Cap'n…" He then reluctantly lowers his aim. "We don't have a chance at this with only the two of us."

"We just have to bide our time…"

Holton mounts, waves a hand, and rides off with the dog following after him. Again, Corky turns back to make a headcount of the number of Comanche assembled at the cave. He peers down the barrel of his rifle and then looks to Bentley. "I hope he finds Jules."

As the ranger captain studies the overwhelming numbers of hostiles, he nods. "Hope is all we have right now."

~*~

Stumbling on uneven footing, Jules slowly leads the young boy through the darkness. They sit to rest, breathing in the damp, stale air. Jules sniffs, and the young boy whispers, "What's that smell?"

"Bat guano, I suppose…"

The two stare into the pitch blackness, silent for a moment as they catch their breath. Seeing nothing and hearing only their labored breathing, the child finally speaks. "Are we lost in here?"

"We're free for now, but it's no use wandering around in the dark if we don't know which way is out."

"The Indians know the way."

"We can't go out that way without being caught again." Jules pinches his nose to stifle the strong stench of the cave. His ears perk to a faraway sound, and he listens… "Do you hear something?" They both listen, until the boy responds, "No. Should we make a fire to see our way through, maybe?"

"They might see it."

The boy sighs and softly adds, "I don't think we have anything to make a fire with anyway."

Staring long and hard into the dark nothingness of the passageway, Jules remarks, "We can sit here and starve, or we keep trying to find a way out."

The young boy reaches out to put his hand on Jules and then whispers, "I'll follow you." They both climb to their feet. Jules feels the boy grasp tightly onto his arm, as they make their way through the obscure blackness.

Chapter 36

Dozens of mounted Comanche begin moving north and away from the underground caves. The two Texas Rangers, Bentley and McCandles, watch them depart with the trailing line of chained captives. Anxious, Corky turns to the captain and questions, "Do we follow after them?" Bentley thinks but doesn't respond. Holding his thumb against the hammer of his cocked rifle, Corky continues. "If enough of them leave, we might be able to get the few left-behind and then get a look inside them caves."

"We'll let Holton Lang take care of the cave and our young friend. We'll follow after the bunch with the captives. With any luck, our fellow rangers will intercept them before they get above the Llano River."

Lowering his rifle, Corky nods his agreement and continues to watch the procession. "Sure hate to leave here without the kid. I hope Holton Lang finds him okay..."

Ranger Bentley looks back to their horses and then down to the war party. "Me, too..." Hunkering down lower, he scoots backwards and moves toward their mounts. "Okay... Let's go after them." Corky gives one last look at the departing Indians, ducks back and follows Bentley.

~*~

Crawling around the stalagmites on the wet rock floor, Jules and the boy slowly make their way. Ahead, there seems to be a glowing light, and Jules blinks several times to see if his eyes are playing tricks on him. Carefully, he reaches back to feel for the boy and then whispers, "Keep quiet now... There looks to be something ahead." Creeping along the floor, the boys come to the intersection of a smaller tunnel that makes a slight turn.

Around the bend, there is a mid-sized cavern with a campfire burning in the center. Staying back, Jules and the boy let their eyes adjust to the light. After a while of observing the chamber, Jules pulls the boy back and quietly speaks to him. "I don't see anyone out there, but if there is a campfire, someone must be tending it. They might be close enough to the outside to gather tinder."

Relief brightens the young boy's features. Excited, he whispers, "I saw two passages on the other side of that cave!"

"Me, too..."

"Should we split up?"

Jules shakes his head. "No..." He pauses to consider. "We should stay together to take on whatever comes."

"Okay..."

"Are you ready?"

"I'll follow you."

"Stay behind me." Jules takes the knife from his pocket, clutches the handle in one hand and holds the boy's small hand with his other. He peeks around the bend of the tunnel to the empty chamber again and sees that no one is around. "Okay... Let's go!" The boys rush out of the passageway and cross the room into the light.

Suddenly, two warriors step out from the dark to block their path.

Above the Llano

Shielding the young boy behind him, Jules brandishes the knife blade out in front of him and takes a step backward. Laughing, the Indians move toward them. One of them holds a tattered bundle of fabric. When the shadows shift, and the light from the campfire shines directly on the piece of clothing in the Indian's hand, Jules quickly recognizes a pattern from a girl's prairie dress.

Immobilized by the trauma of his past, Jules stands stock-still as the Indians advance. When one of the warriors reaches out to take the knife from Jules' hand, the boy behind him pleads, "Do something... Please!" Breaking out of his temporary paralysis, Jules sweeps his foot across the fire and scatters the glowing coals. As darkness consumes the cavern, Jules stabs out with the knife and hears a yelp, as his blade jabs into the flesh of the closest brave.

A blinding flash and the deafening report of a gunshot are quickly followed by the lever-action of a rifle and another loud *bang*. Jules and the boy remain frozen in the middle of the room. They hear the soft tap of booted feet moving across the stone floor. Gripping the handle of the knife blade tightly, Jules calls out. "Hello...? Who's there?!?"

The coals of the fire are scraped together with the edge of someone's boot, and a stick of kindling is placed on top. The boys blindly stare out, until the piece of firewood slowly takes to flame and fills the chamber with an amber glow. Across from them, the fringed buckskin figure of Holton Lang steps forward into the light and lever-cocks his big-loop rifle.

Not able to stop himself, Jules rushes to Holton and embraces him with the enduring love of a long-lost child. "You came for me...?" Holton wraps his arms around the young man and holds him close. They stand embracing, until Holton finally looks down to see the other child staring back.

149

He glances over to the pair of dead Comanche lying on the floor and then down at Jules. "How are you, boy?"

"I'm okay."

"Who's your friend?"

Jules finally releases his grip on Holton and looks back at the young boy. "I don't know his name."

Holton nods and waves the boy over to join them. "Well, come along now, the both of ya... We need to go. Someone might have heard those shots."

Chapter 37

As the afternoon shadows stretch across the rocky terrain. Holton emerges from a crevice under an overhanging boulder. He pushes the thick brush aside, so that Jules and the young boy can follow him. Outside the cave, seated next to Holton's horse, the loyal canine sits panting a greeting. When Jules sees the scruffy dog, he smiles and looks at the animal's leg. "Thanks, Dog… How's the wound?"

The dog whimpers in reply and walks to the boy's side. They move to the horse, and Holton lifts the younger boy up to the saddle. Looking at Jules, he notices some teenage growth since they last saw one another. "Despite these rough circumstances, you look good, boy."

"Thank you, sir."

Holton loads a few cartridges into the side of his rifle from his gun belt. "What now?"

"How do you mean?"

"I ran into two of your Texas Ranger pals at the other end of these caves, and, despite the terrible odds, they're following after this band of Comanche. They intend to rescue the captives."

Jules looks down at the rusty knife in his hand and then back to Holton. "What can we do?"

"I could just take you both to the nearest settlement, or we can do our best to help."

Jules looks at the young child and replies prudently, "We'll follow after the rangers and drop him off at the first homestead we come across."

From atop the horse, the boy looks down at them and shakes his head. "No. I'll follow you."

Holton is impressed with the young boy's grit. Reaching back to his saddle pouch, he retrieves Jules' pistol. He smiles at Jules, as he hands it over. "Sounds familiar…"

Jules takes the gun, checks to see that it's loaded and stuffs the barrel under his belt. "Was I anything like that?"

"More-so…"

They both look to the young boy, and Jules states, "Okay… You can stay with us awhile, until we say different." Holton takes the reins of the horse and begins to lead it away, and Jules follows after, asking, "How are we going to catch them with only the one horse?"

Weaving his way through the rocks and brush, Holton speaks over his shoulder. "Most of 'em are on foot, and we're travelin' light. We'll catch 'em."

"Okay, let's help those rangers the best we can." With a renewed lease on life, Jules tucks his knife away and follows.

~*~

A large band of Comanche travels to the river to make camp on the southern bank and wait for the rest of the war party to catch up. Rangers Bentley and McCandles, observing from a safe distance, stay on their trail.

As the Comanche set camp, the two rangers study a nearby river crossing. Ranger Bentley takes a gander upriver and then studies the terrain downstream. "We need to keep them from crossing the river and fleeing to the north."

"Fleeing? I don't think they know we're after them…"

Above the Llano

"They will, soon enough."

Assessing their disadvantage, Corky tentatively asks, "You thinkin' of circlin' 'round and tryin' to hold 'em?"

"With only the two of us trying to stop them, they could cross and ride over us pretty quick."

Studying the encampment, Corky sighs. "We could try for their pony herd…"

In thought, Bentley chews on his lower lip and nods. "That might slow them down until some help arrives…"

"We don't know if Hobbs is comin' with the cavalry or even if he's still alive…"

Peering into the waning light of day, Ranger Bentley studies the camp's layout and the location of the prisoners. "With just a few more of us, we could ride right in there, scatter them to the wind and grab most of those captives." Without further comment, they continue to study the movement of the Indians. Finally, Bentley takes a breath, glances back to their horses and murmurs, "We'll wait until nightfall, and then try to get closer."

~*~

A small campfire is sheltered from view by a rocky bluff on the banks of the river. Holton sits with Jules and the young boy as Dog watches them from the evening shadows. The natural sounds of the night are comforting to the boys in comparison to the noiseless environment inside the cave. Holton smiles to himself, as he considers his odd mix of company. He sees that Jules clutches the fancy gun to his lap, while the boy watches the river flow. When Jules notices Holton watching him, he asks, "How near are we to that band of Indians?"

"Half a day, most likely… We should catch up to them about the time they cross upriver."

Jules looks to Dog sitting silently on guard at the edge of the firelight. He stares admiringly at the animal and then turns back to Holton. "That dog found you in Arizona?"

"Yep."

"At your ranch there?"

"Yeah."

Jules remembers long-ago travels from the ranch to where they are now. "That's a far piece."

"Yes, it is."

"How was the place on your return?"

Holton thinks back to the odd couple he left behind. His thoughts are muddled by tender thoughts of Alice and conflicted feelings about leaving without his wounded friend. Gazing at the river, he replies, "It was complicated…"

Wanting to ask more, Jules refrains and looks to the rescued young boy instead. "What is your name, boy?"

The boy turns from staring at the river. Blinking his eyes as he looks across the fire, he utters, "William Parker."

After a short silence, Jules follows with, "I'm sorry about what happened to your mother." The young boy nods and turns his gaze toward the low flicker of flames.

Interrupting the awkward moment, Holton speaks to Jules. "When we catch up with those Comanche tomorrow, what are you expectin' to do?"

"Help those Texas Rangers."

"There are only two of 'em."

Jules glances at the boy and then looks back at Holton. "With us, there'll be four."

The boy looks at them both. "I can fight."

Jules smiles kindly at the youngster. "I bet you can, but we'll need you to keep ahold of the horse."

The boy nods sheepishly, and Holton studies Jules a bit before asking, "You joined up with them rangers?"

"Just temporary…"

Holton thinks for a moment, before speaking again. "You're still wanting to find Bloody Ben, I suppose?"

"Yes."

The westerner fondly regards the young man before him and finally utters, "He's dead."

"You kill 'im?"

Holton shakes his head and vividly recalls the image of the dying outlaw in the riverbank cut-out. "No… You did."

Wisps of campfire smoke shift in Jules' direction, as he stares at Holton from across the flames. Glistening tears begin to form in the young man's eyes despite his trying to hold them back. "I want to see him. Will you take me to his body?"

"Might not be there anymore…"

"Why not?"

Seeing the need for closure, Holton studies the youth. "Wild animals and such, or even the river water rising up, could have taken it away."

Understanding, Jules nods his head. He can't help but feel the strange sensation of a burden being lifted from his shoulders. "You sure he's dead?"

Holton notices that the younger boy is listening to their morbid exchange. "It warn't a pretty way to go, if knowin' that makes you feel some better."

"It does…"

"What now for you?"

"We help the Texas Rangers recover those captives."

Holton nods. "And after?"

"I ain't ever thought much farther… Maybe I'd like to go see that ranch of yours again."

Laying a branch across the fire, Holton raises an eyebrow and grimaces. "It's a mite crowded of late, but you'd be welcome."

Jules looks at Holton with curiosity, as his seasoned mentor positions himself on the ground, preparing for sleep. He watches him a while then catches the young boy observing him in a similar fashion. Feeling a weight of responsibility, Jules finally settles down to sleep and the boy does the same. While the crackling fire burns down to embers, Jules speaks. "Thanks, Holton."

Under his hat, Holton rolls his head slightly to the side and murmurs, "What for...?"

"Comin' for me."

Crossing his arms over his chest, Holton smiles a paternal grin and exhales. "Good to see you again too, kid." The stars shine brightly as Jules stares up to the heavens and settles in to get the first restful sleep he's had in a long time.

Chapter 38

As preparations are being made for the river crossing, several braves are assigned to escort the chained captives. When some horseback warriors cross over, it is discovered that a substantial number of ponies are missing from the herd. A murmur of discontent races through the group.

Lying flat on the ground, Ranger Bentley watches the vast procession. He turns to look, when McCandles rides to his concealed position, leaps from his horse and joins him. Bentley gestures to the numerous warriors standing by the riverbank. "Nice job, Ranger." With his rifle held out in front of him, Corky slides in beside Bentley and looks to the camp. "I herded away what ponies I could, but a lot of 'em scattered and drifted back."

"Anyone see you?"

"One of 'em did, but he won't be speakin' of it any."

They watch the group depart with their line of captives. Clutching his rifle, Corky asks, "No luck with the prisoners, Captain?"

"I lingered close by all night but never had a good enough opportunity that wouldn't get a lot of them killed."

Several of the horseless Comanche stand in the shallows of the river waiting for others to make it across.

Sighting down his rifle barrel, Ranger McCandles murmurs, "We could prob'ly use some ol' Reb tactics on 'em and plink a few off from a distance as they go."

The captain shakes his head. "Too risky... I want to recover those captive alive."

Corky continues to aim his rifle at a horseback Comanche standing midstream. "What're yer thoughts?"

"We wait until the main force of the war party is across. When they start to cross the captives, we rush them."

As the chained prisoners are held at the water's edge, most of the bounty is carried across by mounted warriors. Corky lowers the aim of his rifle and calculates the odds. "That'll still leave about half of 'em to deal with."

With a grim sigh, the ranger captain tilts his head. "This is our best chance to save those prisoners." The rangers watch, as the captives are finally ushered into the river. Bentley taps Corky on the arm, and they both slink back toward the horses to mount up.

~*~

Near the river crossing, the mounted rangers recheck their firearms. The sound of brass cartridges sliding into gunmetal foreshadows the upcoming battle. Stoically, Bentley looks at Corky and queries, "You ready for this, McCandles?"

"I sure would like it a hell of a lot better if ol' Hobbs and a passel of rangers was here with us..."

Bentley responds without the slightest hint of humor. "Ranger, I would like it if I could piss beer."

Corky chuckles at the captain's remark and gives his pistol a spinning twirl before gathering up a fistful of reins. "Cap'n, if'n ya did, you know you'd never be rid of Hobbs."

As the rangers tense up, about to spur their animals on, a rustle in the bushes behind them catches their attention. Ranger Bentley puts his hand out to stop Corky and quickly pivots his horse while lifting up his rifle to aim into the brush. "Who's there? Come out and show yourself!"

A young voice calls out. "Don't shoot, boys! It's me!" Eventually, a single horse pokes its nose through the thicket. The rangers stand at the ready, as Jules rides toward them with a young boy seated behind him in the saddle.

Corky whistles through his teeth and shakes his head. "Jules Ward, you're like a damned cat with nine lives."

Both rangers look to the boy mounted behind Jules. Bentley asks, "Who's that with you?"

Jules rides over and stops alongside the two rangers. "This here is Willie Parker. He was one of the captives."

"Got anymore back there that come along with you? We were just about to liberate a few ourselves." Bentley looks over Jules' shoulder to scan the area. "Where's Mister Lang?"

Another rustling sound in the bushes produces Dog. Then Holton follows, responding, "Yeah... I'm here, too."

The Texas Rangers gratefully acknowledge Holton, and Bentley looks back at Jules. "Glad you found one another."

Lowering the aim of his pistol, Corky proclaims, "Luckily, you found us, too."

With a glance down at the dog, Jules perceptively adds, "It weren't no accident. Where are Hobbs and the others?"

The rangers are silent, until Corky replies, "It's just us."

Turning his horse to the river, Ranger Bentley refocuses his attention on the mission. "We would surely enjoy some time to catch up, but we need to recover the captives before they get north of that river."

Holton looks out at the dozens of Indians spread across the water. Wondering aloud, he turns to Bentley. "Your plan was to take 'em all on with jest the two of you?"

With his rifle held across his lap, the captain nods. "We'll do our best with what the Lord provides us this day."

"Prayers here won't help any, and you won't do a lick of good for them hostages by gettin' dead quick."

Ranger Bentley stares off into the distance, as the line of chained captives is ushered through the waist-deep current. "If you have something to say about it, get it out now."

Holton looks to the boys and motions them down. "Hop on down, the both of you. I'm gonna need my horse." The young boy slides off the animal's hindquarters, and Jules dismounts from the saddle. With his big-loop rifle in hand, Holton leaps a foot to the open stirrup and swings a leg over. Mounted, he addresses the rangers. "Give me a few minutes... Then come out a'shootin' like billy-be-jiggers."

Before the rangers can protest, Holton lopes off toward the river. Bentley looks down at Jules and motions him over. "Mister Ward, hand that boy up behind McCandles, and you climb on with me. We'll move in closer and see what your friend Holton Lang has in store for us."

Jules gives the boy a boost up to Corky's saddle. Then, he takes Bentley's offered stirrup and climbs up behind him. As they ride to the river, they can see Holton approaching the Comanche at the water's edge.

Chapter 39

Charging into the shallow waters at the river crossing, Holton gallops toward the Comanche horde. Those that are mid-river continue to cross, but the others on the shoals stop to curiously observe the lone rider's approach. A call of warning is put out as news of the impending encounter quickly spreads.

Holton brings his horse to a splashing halt, puts his rifle across his lap and, in a sign of peace, lifts up his empty gun hand. The mounted warriors leading the captives stare inquisitively at the buckskin-clad rider. Murmuring softly amongst themselves, they peer with suspicion toward the brush-covered riverbank. Finally, one of the braves shouts to Holton in Comanche. "What do you want, white-man?"

Holton replies in the same tongue. "I come in peace and will take those captives in trade for your lives."

Astonished, the Comanche look around and laugh at the notion of giving up their stolen prize. Yelling above the sounds of the flowing river, the nearest warrior challenges, "You speak brave talk for a man alone."

With his hand still raised in peace, Holton confidently states, "I speak the truth."

The majority of the group, having already crossed, waits in silence on the opposite bank. The few warriors remaining to guard the captives whisper among themselves. The foremost Comanche splashes his horse closer and asks, "What do you call yourself, white-man?"

"Holton Lang."

As the captives remain clustered in the river like herded livestock, the mounted braves confer briefly before shaking their heads. One of the braves waves his arm, shouting to inspire fear. "You speak our tongue, Holton Lang, but I no hear big talk of you!"

Holton replies, "I am not a man of talk, but of action."

The warrior responds with a yell, "You go, now!!"

"Leave the white-eye captives and ride away from here, or you will not live to speak my name to others."

The Comanche leading the captives lets the chain fall into the water and grips his Spencer carbine with both hands. Without consulting the others, he screams a war cry and jabs his heels to the flank of his pony. The Indian races forward through the river, and Holton mirrors the charge.

As the riders rush at one another, the Comanche warrior aims his rifle and fires. Holton returns fire, clipping the Indian pony's ear. The Comanche's mount skitters to the side and tumbles into the shallow water, while the Indian uses both hands to work the action of his rifle. Momentarily out of the running fight, the Comanche struggles to get free of his floundering mount.

In one fluid motion, Holton swings the big-loop rifle out to his side and spin-cocks it. As the rifle comes around, he extends it forward to aim at the next oncoming rider and fires. The Comanche takes the bullet strike mid-chest and rolls backward over the flank of his pony. As he rides through the shallows, Holton sees the man tumble face-down in the river.

Above the Llano

He spin-cocks his rifle again, as another warrior fires a shot at him and charges. Slowing his horse, Holton swings his aim out to the side, squeezes the trigger and sends the Comanche cartwheeling into the water. Incensed at seeing their brethren cut down so quickly, the remaining mounted Comanche rush toward the lone aggressor.

As a half-dozen screaming warriors splash toward Holton, two double-mounted Texas Rangers emerge from the bushes along the riverbank. Consecutively firing their guns, the four generate the appearance of strong reinforcements. Sliding his mount down the embankment, Bentley halts his horse at the edge of the river and glimpses over his shoulder. He hollers to the youth holding on to him behind the saddle. "Hop on down and get to those hostages, Mister Ward!"

"Yes, sir!"

With pistol in hand, Jules slips from the horse and runs across the shoreline toward the charging Comanche and the abandoned captives. He cocks the hammer and fires a round that hits one of the horseback warriors. As gunshots from Holton and the Texas Rangers scatter the Indian's charge, Jules runs past the splashing ponies, to the chained prisoners.

Stopping his mount at the top of the embankment, Corky shoulders his rifle and shoots at the horseback Indians. Two warriors charging toward Holton and Bentley receive simultaneous gunshots that knock them from their ponies. The young boy behind Corky clutches tightly to his coat tails, while the anxious horse prances on the unstable footing above the river and nearly slips.

Rushing to the captives, Jules hands his knife blade to a woman bound with leather ties. "Cut yerself loose and then them others, too!" He aims his pistol at the metal shackle that binds one of the captives and shoots to shatter the forged ring. Jules repeats the process down the line. A scream from a female hostage alerts Jules, and he turns to see the rest of the war party riding back into the river to reclaim their prisoners. Frantically, the unbound captives scatter toward the shore.

Holton and Ranger Bentley, followed shortly after by Corky and the young boy, splash their horses toward Jules. Holton extends his hand down, as he passes alongside Jules, "Climb up here behind me, boy!"

Jules takes Holton's hand and uses the horse's forward momentum to swing himself up. Looking downriver to the fleeing captives, he exclaims, "We can't abandon them to be rounded up again!"

As the would-be rescuers splash to a stop in the river, three abreast, Holton spin-cocks his rifle again and responds. "No one is leaving just yet..."

Chapter 40

The bulk of the war party reorganizes on the opposite shore, while several horseback natives charge across the water. When the native riders get mid-stream, the pace of their ponies is slowed by the deeper water. Raising his arm and then lowering it in a sweeping motion, Ranger Bentley bellows, "Rifles! Fire!!"

Following the captain's orders, Holton and Corky squeeze their triggers. Two warriors slump over, as others continue the charge. Bentley lets go a shot from his Winchester, levers it again and hollers, "We need to keep this line of defense and give those hostages a chance to get away!"

As the horses prance and skitter in the river shallows, Holton spins his mount around to face the attackers again. After taking another shot, he levers his rifle. "If we're staying, we need a better place to hold out."

Corky passes the reins of his horse to the boy's hand that clutches at his waist. "Try to hold this horse steady, boy, so I kin shoot straight..." The ranger sends off another shot, cocks his rifle and shoots again.

Several casualties hold the first wave of charging Comanche at bay. Holton fires his rifle, cocks it, and turns his horse broadside, so that Jules can use his pistol, as well.

Ranger Bentley levers his rifle to find an empty chamber, tucks it across his pommel and heads for the riverbank. "Everyone... Let's head for better cover along the shore!"

The captain splashes across the shallows and hops from the saddle to the sandy shore. While tugging his horse up the embankment, he reaches under the flap of his saddlebag for a box of cartridges. As he pulls his horse away from the river, he calls to Corky. "Ranger McCandles!"

With his young passenger holding on, the ranger rides over and climbs his horse up the riverbank. "Yes, sir?"

"Get that youngster to take the horses a safe distance away and hold them!"

After scooting the boy down, Corky dismounts and instructs the boy. "Now, you heard the Cap'n, young fella. Take these horses off to cover." Obediently, the boy grabs the reins of both horses and scampers into the brush.

When Holton rides over to the rangers, Jules slides off. Looking back up to Holton, he declares, "I'll stay here and hold this position while I can."

From his higher vantage point, Holton can see that the hostiles across the river are regrouping for a unified charge. Disheartened, he bows his head at the boy. "Won't last long."

Jules glances to the rangers taking up firing positions behind a tangle of driftwood. "It'll keep longer with me here, and they will do the same."

Holton thumbs out several cartridges from his holster belt and loads them into his rifle. "Yeah, they will at that..."

Gazing up at Holton, Jules respectfully pronounces, "You taught me what I know about friends who are family."

"And what was that?"

The young man spins his pistol on his finger, grips the handle and grins. "Never know where you'll find 'em."

Above the Llano

Holton smiles and then looks over the embankment to something far off. He un-holsters his own sidearm and, with a fancy gun-twirl, tosses it down to Jules. "Make use of this and hold out as long as you can. I'll be back shortly."

Jules watches Holton spur his horse up the riverbank, and the two rangers exchange an unsure glance. When Jules joins them near the driftwood log, he notices that the Indians have already started to cross the river. Moving slowly at first, they gradually pick up speed.

As Holton disappears into the distance, Corky gives a welcome nod to Jules. "Well dang, fellas... Looks like he that rides away can live to fight another day." Jules, with his two pistols, takes a position between the rangers and aims one of the handguns over the log. Corky is glad to have him alongside for the fight. "Hot-damn, here we are once again... Outnumbered, just like at the Alamo."

Looking sidelong at his ranger friend, Jules counters, "Them were Mexicans they fought, not Comanche."

Corky aims his rifle. "I don't speak *Mex* or *Comanch*."

Ranger Bentley squints down his rifle sights toward the oncoming riders and speaks to Jules. "Your friend there is a smart man to run off."

Jules looks at the captain and adamantly proclaims. "Holton Lang never run away from a fight in his life."

Corky glimpses over his shoulder to where Holton departed and turns back to the charging warriors in the river. "Well, it sure do look that way, and I don't blame 'im none."

Jules sights down the barrel of his pistol and, before he pulls the trigger, murmurs, "We'll see..."

Chapter 41

In a flurry of splashing water and bloodcurdling war screams, the Comanche charge across the river. Jules and the two rangers wait until the mounted warriors are almost mid-river before unleashing a volley of gunfire. Several wounded natives fall from their mounts, while the others continue to splash forward. Bentley hollers above the sound of gunfire. "Keep shooting until the last man!"

The ranger captain repeatedly levers his rifle, aims, and snaps off shot after shot, until he clicks on an empty chamber. With the attackers rapidly approaching, and with no time to reload the rifle, he pulls out his sidearm, cocks it, and extends his arm to aim.

Beside him, Jules and Ranger McCandles keep up a steady barrage of shooting. They lessen the number of attackers significantly, but seem unable to stop the charge. Levering his rifle, Corky blows away the smoke that trickles from the open receiver. "Damn, we give 'em a good show... They'll be on us soon!"

Jules fires both of his handguns, until they click empty. Then, he reaches over to slide out a handful of cartridges from Corky's gun-belt. "We ain't licked just yet."

Eric H. Heisner

Astounded, the ranger looks over to Jules and then back at the dozens of screaming Comanche riding at them. "Damned if you don't have the rosiest outlook I ever heard!"

Jules clicks the side gate of Holton's pistol closed, and lifts it as he cocks. He squeezes off a shot and peeks over at the ranger beside him. "N'er can tell..."

Corky's rifle clicks empty, and he draws his pistol out. The three of them continue to fire, until Bentley's sidearm clicks on a spent cartridge. He draws his Bowie knife from his belt and brandishes it. "They're just about on us boys!"

The Comanche are only a few yards away when a screaming holler, like the *Rebel Yell*, erupts from riders behind. The defenders turn to see Ranger Hobbs soaring over the embankment with Holton riding alongside and a posse of riders following at full gallop. With guns blazing, the horsemen rush into the river. Racing through the shallows, with a pistol in each hand, Ranger Hobbs cocks and fires. Riders are scattered in all directions, and the charge is broken.

Returning to the ranger's last defended position, Holton tosses a sack of cartridges to the men on the ground. "Good to see you fellas are still around." He offers a salute to Jules and Captain Bentley before riding off.

Corky stands to cheer his fellow rangers on, waving his gun high over his head. From the midst of the melee, an arrow flies in a graceful arc and pierces his side just above the hip. The ranger looks down at the wooden shaft and drops behind the driftwood cover. Incredulous, he wobbles the arrow that pierces through the fleshy part of his abdomen and curses. "Ahh, dammit... I'm hit!"

Scooting in closer, Jules helps the injured ranger to lie down on his side. Glancing to them as he reloads his pistol, Bentley hollers, "Keep your heads down, boys!" He looks out at the scattered horde of Comanche. "The fight isn't over yet!"

170

Jules notices that the pointed tip of the arrow pushes at the back of Corky's shirt. "You'll be okay, pard... It looks like it passed through without hitting a bone."

Feeling at his back, Corky shakes his head in dismay. "I'm a damn fool for catching one..."

"Fellas much smarter than you have done worse."

The ranger looks at Jules confused, trying to figure out if the remark was a compliment. "Thanks. I think..."

With the attack now dispersed up and down the river, Ranger Bentley reloads his rifle, and watches Ranger Hobbs continue the fight from horseback. He looks at Corky and Jules, as he levers the gun. "You're a good man, Mister Ward. Tend to that man's wound... It will all be over soon."

~*~

Excitement still hangs in the air, as the battle wanes. The posse sent by the settlement sees to it that the rescued captives are gathered together and returned to the riverbank. On the opposite shore, a smattering of Indians makes a hasty retreat with what little bounty they can carry from their raids.

Chapter 42

Lying on a blanket in the ranger camp, Corky McCandles wears a blood-smeared bandage wrapped around his middle. Looking thankfully across the campfire to Jules, he nods and lays his head back to rest. Wincing from the pain in his side, Corky stares upward to the afternoon sky. "Thanks again, kid. For patching me up..."

Dog ambles into the campsite and finds a spot to lounge near Jules. The youth glances at the dog and then looks back to the wounded ranger. With a laugh, he comments, "Corky, you sure did whine and cuss about havin' that Indian sticker in ya a whole lot more'n Dog, here." The ranger looks over at Dog and shakes his head. "Yeah, I prob'ly did, at that. He is one tough ol' critter." Turning onto his good side, Corky looks to a cluster of civilians gathered at another campfire. Heaving a sigh, he reflects. "I'm sure glad not to have gone through what you and them had to."

Lowering his gaze, Jules murmurs, "They are the lucky ones who made it through alive, I suppose..." He can't help but look over to Willie and think of the boy's dead mother lying in the cave and left behind.

The somber moment is interrupted when Holton rides in with Hobbs and Bentley. They dismount and walk over.

Hobbs chuckles, and with the edge of his boot, kicks a bit of dirt toward the recovering ranger. "How'r ya doin' there, Cork-meister?"

Ranger McCandles looks up at them all and grimaces. "As good as can be expected."

Placing a hand on his holstered sidearm, Bentley looks over at the recovering hostages. "We'll stay here the night and ride for Round Mountain in the morning. There, you can rest up more and heal your wound."

Smiling, Corky tries to conceal his pain as he looks up. "We done good by them captives, ain't we?"

Resting on the tips of his spurs, Ranger Hobbs squats by the campfire and lays a stick on top. "We got 'em gathered, and we'll git 'em to where they belong soon enough." With a grateful tilt of his head, the crouched ranger looks at Holton. "We have you to thank, Mister Lang. For what you done..."

"Glad to be of help."

Hobbs digs his boot soles into the soft dirt and grunts, "If I hadn't of recognized Holton 'n followed 'im to the river, things would'a turned out a whole lot different."

As Jules looks proudly at Holton, his frontier mentor, Ranger Bentley nods his appreciation and cordially adds, "Yes, we are indebted to you, sir."

They linger around the glowing fire as evening falls. Two men on night guard stand silhouetted against the sky. Corky sits upright, leans on a bent elbow and turns to Jules. "What is next for you, kid? You still on the hunt after that outlaw, Bloody Ben?"

The young man looks to Holton, and they exchange a look of understanding. Jules turns back to Corky. "Naw... There ain't been word of him since our last meetin' and I don't expect there to be any again."

Above the Llano

Rangers Hobbs and Bentley look on approvingly, and both notice when Holton bows his head as if well-informed. Hobbs adjusts from his squatted position to lean on a knee. "There ain't much long game in jest huntin' a single outlaw. There's too many to keep ya busy jest here in Texas."

With a cunning grin, Jules looks around and replies, "My outlaw hunting exploits could be at an end for now. Could be I'll head further west. Or, maybe up to the mountains of Colorado to see what they're about…"

Tapping Ranger Hobbs on the side with his knee, Bentley tilts his head as a signal to check on the other camps. "We'll see you off in the morning. If you come to Texas again, we'd be happy to have you in our camp anytime."

Hobbs stands, brushes off his pant leg and chuckles. "Havin' a young'un like you 'round, who can shoot and has no fear in the face of them red-devils, sure can make an ol' ranger like me want to reconsider his choice of occupation."

Jules walks over to Hobbs and extends his hand. "Thank you, sir, for bringin' me on."

Hobbs shakes the boy's hand. "It was my pleasure."

Jules turns to Bentley, and the captain nods his support. "You're a good man, Mister Ward." The two Texas Rangers move on attend to others gathered around the various fires, leaving Jules with Holton and Corky, and the young boy. When Jules peers over at the kid, he sees him return the regard with an admiring gaze. "Where are you gonna go?"

Willie shrugs and glances at them around the fire circle. "I ain't never bin to Colorado…"

Surprised, Jules responds, "You don't really think you wanna come along with me?"

"If you don't want me along, I'll jest follow you."

Jules looks up at Holton and then to the dog, seated between them. "How about you, Mister Lang?"

Standing with his big-loop rifle hanging in his hand, Holton looks around the camp circle. His gaze travels from Corky over to the boy, then to the dog, and finally to Jules. "Might like to see some of that mountain country myself."

"What about the ranch?"

"The land will always be there."

"But who will tend to it?"

An impish smile crosses Holton's features at the entertaining thought of Bear being left to be civilized by Alice. "The land can care for itself better'n we ever could. B'sides, Colorado is nearly on the way."

Jules looks across the fire to the boy seated opposite. "Mister Lang, you sure do attract an odd mix of company."

Holton shakes his head and tucks his rifle underneath his arm. "Sorry, kid. He's yours to care for. I done already taught you what I thought I could." Feeling paternal approval from the buckskin-clad westerner, Jules puts a stick in the fire. He looks at the sky and remarks, "There's some time yet 'fore a new day, and I ain't much for sad good-byes... How 'bout we gather our belongings and set out right now?"

Holton looks at Dog, and the canine climbs to his feet. He nods his head to Jules. "I'm game, if you are."

Jules looks to Willie by the fire. "How about you, kid?"

"I'll follow you."

Spread out on his blanket by the fire, Corky waves as they sneak through the camp and head toward their horses. "So long, fellas. It's been, uhh... well... interestin'..."

Turning back, Jules waves. "See ya, pardner. Heal up that wound a your'n, and I'll ride with ya again someday."

"My wife will see to it that I'm nursed well."

"Then, you'll not want to stay put fer long."

"Sure thing. When she gets to chewin' and naggin' me, I'll be out rangerin' again shortly." Corky nods his head and looks across the way to Dog. The canine's eyes glimmer in the firelight then turn away. "Goodbye to you too, ya funny dog." Hitched up on an elbow, Ranger McCandes touches his bandaged side, as he watches the unusual assembly of travelling companions depart.

Mounted on apprehended Indian ponies, with blankets draped over for saddles, Jules and the boy ride from the camp with Dog tagging along behind. Following their lead, Holton trails along with his big-loop rifle cradled across his lap.

The End…

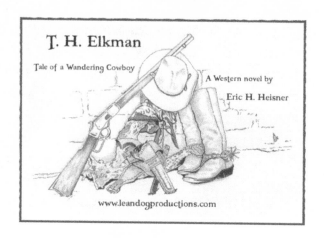

If you enjoyed **Above the Llano**, read other stories by
Eric H. Heisner
www.leandogproductions.com

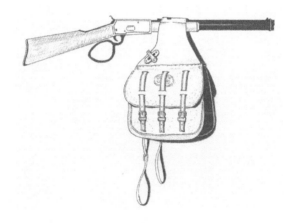

Eric H. Heisner is an award-winning writer, actor and filmmaker. He is the author of several Western and Adventure novels: *West to Bravo, Seven Fingers a' Brazos, T. H. Elkman, Along to Presidio,* and *Wings of the Pirate.* He can be contacted at his website:

www.leandogproductions.com

Al P. Bringas is a cowboy artist, actor and horse lover. He has done illustrations for novels including: *West to Bravo, T. H. Elkman* and *Wings of the Pirate.* He lives and works in Pasadena, California.

CPSIA information can be obtained
at www.ICGtesting.com
Printed in the USA
LVHW101129180522
719077LV00012B/332/J